Psalms 33:13+14
Hebrews 10:17

OMNISCIENT

A novel by David Schmittou

ZOË LIFE
PUBLISHING
WORDS TO LIVE BY

© 2008 David Schmittou

Published by:
Zoë Life Publishing
P.O. Box 871066
Canton, MI 48187 USA
www.zoelifepub.com

All Scripture quotations, unless otherwise indicated, are taken from The New King James Version (NKJV) of the Bible copyright © 1982 by Thomas Nelson, Inc. The Bible text designated (RSV) is from the Revised Standard Version of The Bible, copyright © 1946, 1952, 1971 by the Division of Christian Education of the National Council of the Churches of Christ in the USA. The Bible text designated (TLB) is from The Living Bible copyright © 1971 by Tyndale House Publishers, Inc. Scripture quotations marked (NIV) are taken from the Holy Bible, New International Version ®. Copyright © 1973, 1978, 1984 by International Bible Society. Scripture quotations marked as (NLT) are taken from the New Living Translation Holy Bible. New Living Translation copyright © 1996 by Tyndale Charitable Trust. Scripture quotations marked as (NASB) are taken from the New American Standard Bible copyright © 1960, 1962, 1963, 1968, 1971, 1972, 1973, 1975, 1977, 1995 by The Lockman Foundation.

Author: David Schmittou
Cover Designer: Chamira Jones
Editorial Team: Dr. Robert McTyre, Jessica Colvin

First U.S. Edition 2007 Softcover, Perfect Bound

Library of Congress Cataloging-in-Publication Data

Schmittou, David.
  Omniscient / by David Schmittou. – 1st U.S. ed.
     p. cm.
  ISBN 1-934363-24-3 (softcover)
  I. Title.
  PS3619.C4465O66 2008
  813'.6–dc22
                          2007045612

Summary: A man, just like everyman—a public school educator, a loving husband, and a father of a beautiful son...James discovers an inexplicable room deep within the walls of his basement...

10 Digit ISBN 1-934363-24-3 Softcover, Perfect bound
13 Digit ISBN 978-934363-24-9 Softcover, Perfect bound

For current information about releases by David Schmittou or other releases from Zoë Life Publishing, visit our web site: http://www.zoelifepub.com

Printed in the United States of America

                    # v6 11 26 07

OMNISCIENT

A novel by David Schmittou

Table of Contents

Introduction

Creating a title for this book required a bit of thought before I was finally able to settle on *Omniscient*. The word itself means "all knowing." For many, this title will still seem like a mystery until having completed the story, and possibly reading the afterword; but I am hopeful that by the time you are done, you will begin to understand why I made this selection.

Growing up, I was a fairly shy child. I was nervous in new surroundings and around new people. Being the center of attention was never something I sought out. I hated the thought of a group of people looking at me. In school, speeches and presentations terrified me. I recently heard of a study that reported findings that made me feel as though I was not alone in this. Apparently public speaking is the number one fear among Americans, beating out even death.

For me, there was just something nerve racking about the idea of people watching me. I can remember lying in bed numerous nights, unable to fall asleep, because I was sure that as soon as I did drift off, someone was going to sneak to my window and just watch me lie there.

The fear of being seen is prevalent in society today. Nowadays I take my son to the park. Playing around us there are always kids slightly older than him. As I stand by him and "overprotect" him, I notice that most of the other parents are either buried in a book, oblivious to what is going on, or not even present. Every once in a while in the midst of play, I will hear a kid let an obscenity fall out of his mouth. Finding the kid who said it, I have recently begun to notice a trend. The kid's first impression is never to apologize to those nearby, but instead to look around and see if his mom or dad happened to notice. If they did, the kid will normally quickly try to make remedy of the problem; if not, he will continue on as if he did nothing wrong. It's as if he is only guilty of doing something wrong if his mom or dad says so...or more appropriately if they catch him.

This type of behavior is not only characteristic of kids. Drive down any interstate during rush hour and you can witness the same behavior amongst adults. Cars zoom buy at eighty miles an hour, but up ahead they all begin to flash their brake lights. As you approach the location, you see a police car parked on the side of the road with a radar gun pointed out of the window. The drivers know they are breaking the law and that is why they tap their brakes, but the only thing that brings them back into obedience of the law is the idea of being seen by a police officer who has the power to issue a ticket.

It seems like even Hollywood has caught onto the idea of people secretly watching other people. Movie after movie is produced telling the story of a secret agent who uses his new gadget to spy on a bad guy and save the world. The news media today reports on a daily basis how American's rights are supposedly being violated by criminals tapping into our private information on the internet, our government conducting searches without warrants, etc. It seems that wherever we turn we are reminded that we are being watched.

This book does not try to discredit this idea. In fact its primary focus is to reinforce it. My goal is to try and remind each of us that we are being watched. We are being observed. You are, in fact, this very moment being observed by a force that is *omniscient*.

Chapter One

It was another warm Sunday morning as James Carlise tried to fasten his seatbelt as quietly as possible. His sixth month old son had fallen asleep in the arms of the church's nursery worker and James had no desire to wake him from his nap unnecessarily. Strapped into his safety seat in the back, Travis had only been sleeping fifteen minutes, and needed at least another thirty-five minutes to avoid waking up grumpy and thus ruining what had the potential for being another restful end to the weekend.

James and his wife, Christy, spent every Sunday going through the same routine. This week, the church's pastor had spoken about something James was already having a difficult time remembering. As a member of the usher staff, James had spent the majority of the service collecting the offering, creating receipts, escorting kids to their own special wing of the building, and shaking hands with some of the more distinguished members. He did, however, insure that he was able to enter the sanctuary before the congregation was dismissed so that the pastoral staff could see him with his arm around his wife in the last pew, playing the part of a man with all of his priorities in order. With his short black hair styled perfectly so that his bangs fell to a point just above his eyebrows and his dark conservative suit contrasting with his wife's new summer dress and long blonde hair, James and his wife Christy, even while seated in the last row, were the stand-outs of the assembly. As they pulled out of the parking lot in their new Chevy SUV, James instinctively hit the button to turn on the Sirius Satellite Radio he had grown to depend upon. How he made it with the simple AM/FM radio he had in all of his previous automobiles he had no idea. When the salesperson at the dealership had offered this upgrade at no extra cost, James had been skeptical of its true value, but had since grown to love the wide variety of commercial free choices he could choose to listen to. Along with the radio, this SUV had been equipped with a sound system that allowed passers-by to hear the bass from a block away when turned to the proper level. Today, however, with Travis sleeping in the back, and a line of cars following him from the church parking lot, James made sure that his speakers were producing a more appropriate decibel. The station being listened to was one of Christy's favorites as it always conjured up memories of when the couple had met in college fifteen years ago. Preset on his dashboard with the number one button, James made sure that this station was only listened to when Travis was sound asleep as the topics of sex, drugs, and alcohol that were being sung about were too mature for such an innocent little baby boy to hear.

Ten minutes after pulling out of the parking lot of Divine Hope Church, the young family was entering the garage attached to their four-bedroom home in a new community that their friends jokingly referred to as *Pleasantville*. Pulling Travis out of his seat in the back, James delicately cradled his son, took him to his jungle themed room and placed him gently in his white slatted crib.

With Christy downstairs working on a quick breakfast, James decided to head to his bedroom to change from his heavy wool suit and into a more comfortable sweat suit. As was his custom upon entering any room in the house, his first action was to locate the remote control and turn on the TV. Too much quiet led to too much time for reflection after all.

As the light from the screen began to slowly brighten the room, James heard the voice of Tim Russert interviewing a panel of guests on this week's edition of a popular political news program. Without paying too much attention to the details, James heard the pundits discussing the hottest new scandal to plague the White House. He wasn't aware of all of the technicalities, but the guests on the TV seemed to claim the President had violated the Constitution by allowing the FBI, CIA, or some such agency to eavesdrop on the phone calls of select Americans without obtaining a warrant. Never being extremely gifted in understanding the political structure of America, James felt he was doing his part as a citizen by watching Russert interrogate a host of who's who each week.

Today's discussion brought James' memory back to a time when he was known as Jimmy. At seventeen years old, Jimmy was not the best student in his senior class, but he always loved school, especially when he was lucky enough to have teachers like Ms. Mason.

Ms. Mason was a first year teacher fresh out of college. Teaching senior English at Westchester High School, she was barely four years older than some of her students. To remove some of the awkwardness that resulted from such a small age gap, she encouraged some of her students to call her by her first name, Samantha, Sam for short. James was one of those students.

During that year, Sam had encouraged Jimmy to run for Student Council President, a position he was eventually elected to. Being the staff sponsor for the Student Council, Sam often met with Jimmy outside of school to discuss homework assignments and school functions. Sometimes when he was lucky enough to get her mind off of school, topics like music, romance, and life dreams trickled their way into their discussions as well.

It was at one of those meetings that Jimmy experienced his first wine cooler, his first cigarette, and his first kiss. Although he was sure that Sam never really thought of him as more than a student, and without the case of Bartels and James they had enjoyed, nothing physical would have ever happened, that evening did wonders for elevating his self confidence and his desire to succeed in English. In fact, looking back on it, she was probably the person most responsible for him choosing to go into the field of education.

When he began his first year at college he never even considered the idea of working in a school for the rest of his life. During a speech class that he was required to take as a part of the university's general curriculum however, he realized how much he craved being the center of attention. While the other students were agonizing over the idea of speaking in front of their peers, he was finding himself more and more excited each time he was given the chance to stand in the front of the room. Having all eyes on him was a rush. Knowing that if he did really well, the professor would state in front of everyone that he was doing a great job. That was more of an inspiration to succeed than actually earning credit for the course. It was the same way in high school. Hearing Sam utter her approval in front of everyone had driven him to impress. Now on a daily basis, he was asking kids to do the same for him.

Towards the end of his senior year, once "senioritis" had already begun to take its effect on her classes, Sam assigned the George Orwell classic *1984* to her group of seventeen-year-olds. Still eager to impress his crush, James read through the novel in two nights. During fifth period, his hand was always the first in the air when his class was invited to share its feelings on "Big Brother," invasion of privacy, and similar topics. Knowing how embarrassed he would be and how devastated Sam would be if their secret relationship was ever revealed, James always displayed passionately his belief that people should be allowed to maintain a sense of secrecy in their lives.

The government, in his mind, spent too much time trying to control its citizens. If a person wanted to smoke marijuana in his own house that he paid for, whose business was it? If a person wanted to spend all of his money getting drunk at home and passing out in his bed, who cared? If a person wanted to spend all of their time and money calling 1-900 numbers to get their fortune read to them, nobody needed to know. If people wanted to smoke cigarettes and supply minors with wine coolers, who cared? People were entitled to a private life.

Today as he watched the TV in his bedroom, it appeared to him that Orwell's book was coming true. What at one time was only viewed as science fiction was now a reality being discussed by some guy from the CIA before a national audience. He was arguing that what had been done was all in the name of national security, but James thought he knew the truth. It was just another ploy by the government to get involved in regulating the morality of its citizens. If the government could find out what people were up to when the lights were out and doors were closed, it could pass more laws against whatever actions were taking place. It could then make more arrests and issue more tickets. This would raise more revenue for the bureaucrats and give the politicians one more thing to take credit for as they quoted the number of criminals they were able to remove from the street. Couldn't the government use his tax dollars on things more constructive than watching the every move of its citizens?

Chapter Two

Monday morning came and James woke up at his usual five o'clock. He didn't have to be to Miller Middle School, where he served as assistant principal, until seven thirty but he enjoyed having some alone time before hitting the road. Work was a place where James spent most of the day trying to correct the actions of kids who came from clueless parents. He knew society as a whole had gotten itself stuck in an interesting paradox. Parents no longer had the time or desire to teach morality to their children at home. Instead, they expected the schools to do all of the dirty work; but if a student was being held accountable for his actions in a classroom, it was a common occurrence for those same parents to claim that the school had overstepped its bounds. He felt many days like he was fighting an uphill battle. The hour he gave himself each morning was often the only time he had all day to be alone.

With his son and wife both sound asleep upstairs, James liked to use this time to catch up on the latest sports scores by watching the reruns of last night's *Sportscenter*. Being late May, the NFL season was only a memory as were his hopes of his favorite NBA and NHL teams advancing deep into the playoffs. His favorite baseball team had last night off and as a result, this addition of highlights did little to catch his attention.

Having received an offer from his cable TV provider last week to get a package of premium movie channels for free for the next six months because he was, in their words, a "valuable customer," James decided to see if there were any brainless adventure movies on at this hour of the morning.

The first three channels he tried were showing romantic comedies that were quickly dismissed. The fourth channel, however, did have something on that sparked his interest.

The cable company he used provided a feature in which every time a channel was changed the viewer could get a sampling of information on the show currently being viewed. The particular movie on display right now had an information listing that caused James to stop flipping channels. The name of the movie was *Sorority House*. According to the screen, the movie contained sexual content, nudity, and adult themes—not quite what he began looking for, but... something definitely worth a peek. Setting the remote control down, he got comfortable in the La-Z-Boy recliner he had owned since his college days. After glancing quickly to ensure that the living room blinds were still shut tightly, he looked back at the screen in time to see three young blondes engaged in rather lewd acts.

He watched intently for about ten minutes before being brought back to his reality by the faint cries of his son coming from the baby monitor placed on top of the entertainment center. Turning the TV back to ESPN, he then changed the channel one more time to CNN so that the "previous channel" button on his remote would not in some way incriminate him by switching back to scenes similar to ones he had just witnessed.

Christy stayed home with Travis all day, but James often

got him out of his crib in the morning so that she could sleep in a little bit. Knowing if he waited too long Christy would get up to see what was wrong, James sprang up the stairs two at a time and entered the door into Travis's jungle. Peering over the railing of the crib, James locked eyes with his beautiful boy. His crying instantly ceased and a wide grin formed on the baby's face. Opening the room's blinds, the first rays of sunlight could be seen creeping over the horizon.

James delicately undressed his son, changed his diaper, and placed his newest "onesy" over his little body. Having completed all of the maintenance that his little guy required, James scooped him up and carried him downstairs.

Entering the living room, James was immediately filled with a sense of panic. Sitting on the couch was Christy, her hair disheveled, wearing one of his old oversized t-shirts, with a dazed look on her face, but still looking gorgeous even at this time of the morning. What was she doing up? What was she looking at? Had he forgotten to change the channel? Was she staring at one of his little secrets?

"Good morning. What are you doing up?" he asked, trying to read her expression.

She made no reply.

"What are you watching?"

"Oh, morning," she finally responded. "I was just watching the reporters on CNN rip apart our President. They're all saying this wire tap thing is going to ruin his legacy."

"Really?" James questioned followed by a deep sigh.

So he *had* changed the channel. She was just trying to focus on the political jargon being thrown around over cups of coffee the newsmen had been given as props.

"I guess you need to consider the source," he continued. "Remember Pastor John says CNN can't really be trusted anymore. All they ever do is look for a way to criticize the White House."

Walking out of the room and sighing once more, James set Travis on the floor and quickly surrounded him by a small mountain of mirrors, rattles, and stuffed turtles.

This wasn't the first time he had done some before-the-dawn girl gazing, but this had to be the last. Each time he had justified it to himself with an excuse and today had been no different. He hadn't really been looking for that kind of entertainment. After all his son and wife had been upstairs. He was just channel surfing and got a little curious.

Today, however, he felt a little guilty. When he came down the stairs with his son in his arms and saw his wife sitting there watching TV, wearing his clothes, and looking so distraught and confused, he felt the way he had when he was twelve and his mom walked in on him having a secret conversation on the phone in his room with the girlfriend he was not allowed to have. His parents had forbid him from having a girlfriend until he was fifteen. At the time he didn't agree with the rule; he didn't understand the rule, but when he turned around just after telling the girl on the other end how much he loved her and saw his mother standing in the doorway, he knew he was in trouble. He tried to explain himself. He had a good excuse, but even as he tried to justify his actions he knew he had been wrong.

This was similar to how he felt today. As he looked at Travis playing and his wife smiling, he felt like he had let them down. Thank God he had changed channels before running upstairs.

He could not begin to imagine the embarrassment he would have felt if his secret had been found out.

Chapter Three

Late May in a middle school is not necessarily one of the world's calmest locations. In the five years since he had achieved the position of assistant principal James had asked himself at least one hundred times if he had made the right career move. When he first made the decision to leave his classroom behind and move into the small windowless space tucked into a corner of the main office, many of his colleagues had joked that he had moved over to "The Dark Side." Transitioning from a world of creating lesson plans, grading papers, and parent teacher conferences to one in which he was given a pay raise, a name plate above his door, and his own secretary at first appeared to be a wise move. Mondays in May, however, made him second-guess himself.

Aside from his role as the school's chief disciplinarian, he was also charged with the task of performing evaluations on all of the teachers in the social studies and language arts departments. Having already completed his round of classroom visits, his next task was to perform one-on-one conferences with all of the teachers whose rooms he had visited and give them an honest assessment of his observations.

Normally the conversations consisted of nothing more than

a handshake, a "good morning," and a quick catch-up on the family life of one of the twenty teachers who still taught at Miller when he was a seventh grade English and drama teacher. The meetings scheduled for Monday, however, he believed would be a little different. He still wasn't sure if he was becoming a more stringent evaluator of talent or if the staff was just now becoming a little too comfortable around him, but this year he had paid a visit to the classrooms of two teachers in particular that seemed to be, in his opinion, chaotic and on the verge of out of control. An evaluation conference in the past would have lasted an average of ten minutes, but for each of the first two scheduled this year, James had made sure his secretary allotted at least half an hour.

As Jack Finiden entered the eight by eight foot office, James could already feel the tension. Normally these meetings would take place in the teacher's lounge, a location far more comfortable than the small confines he was normally forced to work in. For a reason that Jack was beginning to suspect however, he had been asked to report to the crowded box that belonged to Mr. Carlise. As the school's union representative and the language arts department's most senior teacher, having taught for twenty-eight years, Jack knew it was well within the power of an administrator to call a teacher into his office, but he also knew it was quite irregular.

In his almost three decades of teaching, Mr. Finiden had only been summoned to the office four times. The initial time was during his first year teaching when he forgot to enter semester grades onto the report cards of two honor roll students. Normally a mistake like that would have been easily remedied, but as Jack still believed, the parents of those two kids had done all of the work for their kids that year and were anxious to find out how they had performed. Being a man who had grayed prematurely, he often felt he was the target of unnecessary harassment. During that first year after college, he already had a head of hair the color of ash and the kids had played on that by often referring to him as "Fireplace Head." Although the students had always made comments like that supposedly behind his back, he had heard some of them and this led him to begin his teaching career on the offensive. Instead of backing down when confronted with a challenge, he had become a teacher bent on showing his students, and their parents, that he was a fully capable teacher, regardless of the names they called him. It was his goal to show them that he was in charge of his room and what happened there—no one else.

The second time he had received his summons was about ten years ago. As the chairman for the language arts department, he was responsible for dispensing a small amount of funds amongst his teachers. That year he had misplaced a little bit more than one hundred dollars. When called to the office to account for the missing funds, no explanation could be given. As a reprimand, he had been stripped of his position as department chairperson to be replaced by the new go-getter, James Carlise.

Before James had called him down this morning, the last time he had been asked to report to the office was five years ago. At that time James Carlise had just notified the department that he would be stepping down from his position to accept his current role as assistant principal. He notified the staff that his old position would be posted and if anyone was interested in filling it, they simply needed to write him a letter of intent explaining their qualifications so that a decision could be made quickly.

After two weeks, Jack was notified that he had been the only person to submit a letter of interest. He was asked to come to the office the next day for what he believed would be a congratulatory meeting. Jack arrived the next day to find he had been mistaken. Not only was he being denied an opportunity to have his old position back, the snotty former "teacher of the year" winner sitting across from him had the nerve to tell him that he did not believe he had the energy level necessary to adequately handle the job, as if James Carlise did. He was told the position would remain unfilled until the proper candidate could be found. Two years passed before anyone filled the vacancy. The woman finally given the job was a third year teacher who had the reputation amongst the female staff as being a suck up, by the male staff of being a real take charge kind of girl, but amongst the male students she had the reputation of being a real "hottie." Jack had a feeling that the later opinion was also shared by James and that her blonde hair and flirtatious personality were probably the real reasons she had been given the elevation in status.

That meeting, half a decade ago, was not the beginning of the lack of trust shared between the two men, but it did not help the situation either. Ever since James began as a teacher in the building ten years ago, the pair often found themselves in heated competition and debate. Whether it was playing in a staff basketball game or at a Monday after school staff meeting, kind words were rarely exchanged. Walking into the office, Jack knew that this meeting would be conducted in much the same way.

Jack Finiden began teaching in an era when it was not uncommon for teachers to intimidate and humiliate students who chose not to show the expected level of respect. He still told stories of the "good ole days" when he was free to call a student to the front of the classroom, have him bend over, and then spank him with the ruler because the child decided to roll his eyes at him when he was in the process of assigning homework. Back then he would say, "The parents not only supported that level of discipline, they encouraged it."

It was no secret that he was not finding as much enjoyment in the new model of education that was being pushed upon him more and more as of late. Instead of being able to run his class like a monarchy, he was feeling more like a mere representative who had to answer to the every wish and command passed his way from parents and administrators alike. Rumors had started to circulate recently that he was eyeing retirement at the end of the year. As was often the case with anyone nearing the completion of a chapter in his life, Jack was apparently trying to make his mark and create a legacy that would not be easily forgotten.

On almost a weekly basis this year, parents and students were making trips to the office of James Carlise to voice some sort of complaint against the aging teacher. Some complaints were fairly minor such as the one brought in by a tiny sixth grader named Tim Dopeney. He claimed Mr. Finiden was being mean to him by refusing to call him by his first name. Instead he decided to call the child by his own unique pronunciation of his last name making it sound more like the name of a dwarf in a Disney movie.

Other complaints were more serious. Some dealt with his

refusal to teach required curriculum, others dealt with his flat out bullying behavior towards his students and sometimes even other staff members. Once rumors of Jack's impending retirement hit his office, James decided he would dismiss most of the claims and just bide his time until the old man left on his own; but after the observation James had made of his classroom, he knew that staying silent was no longer an option.

As Jack entered the office, he knew that this meeting would cover more ground than just the one lesson James had chosen to observe. Because he had almost twenty years more experience, he had refused to ever call his boss by anything other than his first name. He was still a kid compared to him after all. Mr. Carlise was the name the students could call him, but he was James to him. As Jack began his strut across the tile floors that were in desperate need of a new coat of wax, James could hear by the force of each step being taken that Jack was in another one of his moods.

Trying to initiate a peaceful proceeding he began, "Good morning Mr. Finiden. Thank you for taking the time to come in this morning. Your commitment to becoming a good teacher is evident with this sacrifice." James spoke out while shutting the door to begin the meeting. Even as the words were coming out, he could tell Jack knew that he was just spewing forth superficial fluff to get the conversation flowing.

"Jimmy, let me start if I may. First of all, I already am a great teacher. I have been a great teacher since the time you were still clinging on to your mom, letting her know that you had wet the bed again. I know you did not ask me here so that you could tell me how much potential I have. Why don't you cut to the chase and tell me what's on your mind."

"Well Jack, I first need to ask you to keep this a little bit more professional. I think we will both acknowledge that we are not the best of friends and that neither of us will be inviting the other over for coffee any time in the near future, but we can still keep this cordial."

As both men sat in their faux leather rolling chairs staring at each other, James continued, "As you know, I came into your room during third period last Tuesday. While there I saw some really great things, but there were also some things that brought me some concern."

"Really?" Jack interrupted. "Can I ask you what brought you such concern that you were willing to wait almost a week to discuss it with me?"

"Jack, please remember the goal of this meeting is to find ways for us to help our kids succeed even more than they already do. As I said, I saw some amazing things in your class, but I was a little concerned with how you treated some of your students."

Once again Jack interrupted—this time rising to his feet as he did so. "I think you hit it right on the head Jimmy. Those are my students. It's my responsibility to teach them. It's my job to get results from them. I am not sure what has you so concerned, but my students all know my expectations, and know what the consequences will be if they fail to perform to my standards. I am sick of people sticking their noses where they don't belong and trying to tell me how to do my job. If you think you know so much about what goes on in my room why don't you…"

With his face changing to a darker shade of red, James interjected, "Mr. Finiden, I am sure that your students are academically successful, but I am concerned for their emotional well being. What I am about to say is not a judgment on your teaching ability, but instead some constructive criticism based on my own observations.

"While I was in your room I witnessed you raise your voice to three students, tell one student that he asked a stupid question, and as I was leaving the room you called another young man, who quite frankly was acting a little squirrelly, an idiot. I am concerned, Mr. Finiden, that if you speak to kids in that manner when I am present, I am not sure how you speak to them when I am not around. This year I have spent a great deal of my time defending you to angry parents. It's just a misunderstanding, I always tell them. Now I am not so sure it is."

Jack sat back down slightly dumbfounded. A second later he had gathered his thoughts and was back on his feet.

"Mr. Carlise," Jack said for the first time in his life, "I allow you into my classroom because my union tells me I have to. I allow you to judge me, or evaluate me, as you call it because my contract tells me I have to. This does not mean I support it. I am a good teacher. My kids learn. My kids respect me. What I do in my classroom to accomplish these results is my business. I'm going to let myself out now. Feel free to document this meeting in my file. I'm sure you'll say I was flagrant and rude, but remember that is how you perceive it, not me. I consider it honest."

The framed teaching certificate nailed to the wall next to the door shook as the door slammed behind Jack Finiden on his way out of the office. *Why can't people just understand it is my job to try and find ways for them to improve? It's not like going into classrooms and watching other teachers lecture a class is a real pleasurable experience. I am just trying to make them better teachers. Why can't they get that?* James asked himself.

When kids came to see him, they seldom understood that the consequence that was being passed out was designed to change their behavior. Parents seldom supported his conclusions arguing more and more that it was not his place to discipline their kids. Apparently they felt that if their child was reprimanded, it would indicate a deficiency on their end to be effective parents, and as they saw it, that just couldn't be the case. Now it appeared that even teachers on his own staff were rebelling against his authority.

It was only eight thirty in the morning on a Monday. What a start to the week! James decided to have his secretary call his next appointment, Mrs. Jones, in her classroom and tell her that there was no need for her to come down. He would stop by her room later in the day to briefly discuss the great job she had done last week. Although this was not quite true...

It was already late May. If he could just bide his time for a few more weeks and not ruffle any more feathers, the kids, the angry parents, and the teachers would all be gone. He could mind his own business until the end of the school year, and then he would have three months to himself in relative solitude. He would stop by periodically throughout the summer to catch up on unfinished projects, but most of his time would be spent at home with his own family enjoying the company of two people that actually liked having him around—his wife and child.

Chapter Four

Monday afternoon drives were normally something James did not look forward to. He hated manipulating the roads that were jammed with drivers that were too caught up with their cell phone conversations to notice the traffic signals changing in front of them. More and more people were now getting distracted by their new navigational devices and were being forced to make last minute lane changes and turnarounds as they realized their new toy was only helpful if they actually watched the road, and all of the teenagers making him feel like he was in a real life game of *Frogger,* driving too fast and reckless to feel safe, was not what he enjoyed after a long day at school. Today, however, James had a passion to hop into his new SUV, turn on his radio, and settle into a zone all to himself.

After turning onto the main thoroughfare connecting the town James called home, and the city he grudgingly worked in, James decided to turn on a little talk radio. He knew the political shows would all be debating the same stories he saw on TV the day before. Sports radio was more his cup of tea.

At this time of the year, the hosts on the local channels always tried to stretch their creativity to the max as it seemed like there were no actual sports being played in the city. To keep their listeners entertained, the jockeys often resorted to crude games, jokes about women, and other lame attempts to please the audience. Looking for something a little more stimulating, he turned on his satellite radio and began scanning for a station from one of the nation's larger markets. A few seconds into his search, James's fingers pulled away from the dashboard as his ears perked up on a topic he found interesting each time it was debated. The hosts of this show were debating the topic of whether female reporters should be allowed access into the locker rooms of male professional athletes.

One host, a man who was being referred to as "Rich the Pitch," argued, "Women in no way should be given admittance into 'the holy sanctuary of man-dom.' This was a place where men could be men and do men things. No man when half naked and in the presence of a woman, especially a beautiful woman like the TV networks seemed to be recruiting regularly now, would be able to act like himself. Even a happily married man, with kids at home, would put on a show to impress. If the job of a reporter is to get the truth, how can you expect to get anything resembling honesty when a man is forced to put on an act the whole time?"

"The Fat Man," his co-host, responded by pointing out that taking a stance like the one "The Pitch" had just outlined put the media in a precarious position. "Pretty soon all reporters will be removed from locker rooms. Then they will be stopped from conducting half-time interviews, and eventually even post game press conferences will come to an end because often athletes these days are making comments stemming from their emotions. They make a statement and then two days later they're forced to apologize because they offended somebody. After all, what they were quoted as saying was not what they meant. They were just caught up in the moment. If reporters could just give athletes more space and let them play their game, everyone would be happier."

The Fat Man continued, "Nobody wants a world like that. People like the drama. People want to see what's going on behind closed doors, especially if there's a scandal to witness. If putting someone in an awkward position encourages this sort of drama, the American people are happy. After all, look at all of the Reality Shows popping up on TV."

The debate continued as callers from across the country phoned in their opinions and James began to mentally fade out of the conversation. Absorbed in his memories of the day, his car instinctively turned off of the main road and into his subdivision. As he approached his driveway, he was brought back to reality by pushing the button on the remote control that opened his garage door. Reaching down to turn off the radio, he noticed something he had never seen before.

Located immediately to the left of the dial he had used to select his new radio station was a small, very subtle light. Upon first noticing it he thought it might have just been a reflection of the sun pouring in off of the rear window, but as he proceeded to maneuver his car up the twisting driveway, he saw that the light did not move with the sun's position. It remained exactly where he had first noticed it.

Further glances made him believe the light was probably associated with the satellite system, maybe a power indicator. Turning the radio back on he anticipated the light to fade or perhaps change colors from the faint green it currently was, but there was no change. Pulling to a stop inside his garage, James began to suspect the light was associated with the automobile's ignition controls. Thinking the light would fade as the keys were pulled from the steering column, James continued to be puzzled as the engine stopped rumbling yet the light continued to send a faint glow over his seat.

Not wanting to waste his entire evening in the car tracking down the source of a light that appeared to have no meaning, James vowed to himself to look in the owner's manual in the future to see what he could figure out.

As he climbed out and shut the door, James was not aware that the light on his dashboard slowly dimmed while a new one began to illuminate, this one inside his house on the stereo in the living room just a few feet from where James had already sat back with his feet up clutching onto that afternoon's newspaper.

At three o'clock in the morning, James was startled awake. The dog across the street was barking again at some unseen assailant, probably a firefly or mosquito that had come too close to his front door. Before drifting back asleep, James took a customary look at the clock resting just out of arm's reach on his nightstand. The check of the clock was not so much an effort to establish the time, but to ensure that there was indeed a small red dot illuminated in the corner of the digital display indicating that the alarm was still set. He had never been diagnosed with any mental disorders, but his wife had often joked that in this regard he did suffer from Obsessive

Compulsive Disorder. Extremely judgmental of others who arrived tardy to events, James often spent ten minutes prior to falling asleep each night checking and rechecking to make sure that he would be awakened at the designated time by a series or piercing buzzes.

The clock did have the appropriate extra dot so James stuck his right arm under his pillow and prepared to fall back asleep. As he shifted his position to one more comfortable for sleeping he glanced at something that was out of place resting on the small picture frame also situated on the nightstand.

At this early hour of the morning he could not quite make out what the object was, but it appeared to have a faint glow, a light in fact. A small green light. Not wanting to wake Christy who was sleeping soundly next to him, he chose not to turn on his lamp. Deciding the glowing object was probably a figment of his imagination generated by the events earlier in his day, he closed his eyes to fall back asleep. If the object was still there when his alarm clock woke him up in two hours, he would investigate it then.

Unfortunately the early morning wakeup had left him still feeling exhausted at five thirty when the piercing buzzer next to his head woke him up, and he had already forgotten all about it.

Chapter Five

Having survived the final weeks of the school year, James awoke on Friday, June 6th knowing that if he could make it through the day he would have the next three months to get some real work done without 750 kids hustling up and down the hallways every forty-five minutes. His wife, Christy, always knew the last month of school was a chaotic time, but the abbreviated schedule her husband was able to negotiate during the summer months made it all worthwhile. Growing up in a family that would rival any that had been displayed on the TV shows of the 1950's, she loved and valued her family. She had been raised by a mother and a father who had been married for almost thirty-five years now. With only one other sibling to rival for their attention, she was granted the, what was now becoming an ever rarer, commodity of having two people to love her and care for her all though her childhood. Using the model her parents had presented for her, she was committed to seeing her son grow up in a similar environment.

Towards the end of the previous school year, the couple had gotten into a small disagreement when James came home and told Christy that he was joining a golf league, which would require him to play eighteen holes every Wednesday during the months of June and July. In her mind, she simply saw his new commitment as another excuse for him to leave the house for five hours a week. Being an average golfer at best, James tried to convince his wife that joining the league, which was filled with other administrators from local districts, would not only help his handicap, but hopefully his career as well.

What had upset Christy the most was not the idea of her husband off playing golf with the guys once a week; it was the idea of him having a good time without her. Having just discovered that she was three months pregnant with the couple's first child, Christy had dreamed of spending as much time as possible enjoying her last summer with her man, just her man. She knew the following summer would be spent changing diapers and figuring out nap schedules, so she wanted to live it up while she could.

To reach a compromise, and end what Christy had called a highly audible discussion, James had promised to make the golf league a one-year commitment. The next year, he swore, would be devoted to being a husband and father, doing whatever it was that she wanted.

The next year had arrived. She knew that at three o'clock James would officially be on his summer schedule. He could go into the office whenever he thought it was necessary, but could also stay home whenever she wanted him to. For the next ninety days she would have her groom back. He would not be obligated to attend any band concerts and listen to twelve year olds squeak their way through *Twinkle Twinkle Little Star*. He would not have to attend conferences enduring the rants of angry parents claiming he was unfair. This summer he would be all hers. If Travis woke in the middle of the night, he could go check on "the little man." If she wanted to go out for pizza, he could take her.

Traditionally on the last day of school, James stood in the bus loop and waved good riddens to the kids as they ventured home and away from him at 2:50 pm. An hour later he was in his car and pulling into his garage by 4:30 pm. If that held true, she would only have to wait nine more hours and he would be all hers.

Chapter Six

Being the last day, many teachers chose to use their class periods to grade final exams and begin to enter comments on their students' report cards while the kids spent the time signing yearbooks and saying goodbyes. This made it a light day in the office. Aside from sending an eleven-year-old home early for writing obscenities in a classmate's yearbook, Mr. Carlise had not had any kids come to see him today to receive a consequence for their actions.

Never one to let an opportunity pass him by, James decided to take advantage of his unusually slow day by packing up some of his desk clutter that would not be needed until after Labor Day. Beginning with filing stacks of paperwork into a large metal file cabinet in the corner, James then set to tackle organizing documents he had saved into various folders on his computer.

Three hours after starting his crude attempt at organization, Mr. Carlise was finally able to see some fruits of his labor. With a full wastebasket in one corner and a jammed filing cabinet in another, James reached under his desk to shut down his computer for the final time this year.

Leaning over, he stretched his right arm searching for the large plastic tower that housed his hard drive. At some point during the cleaning he must have inadvertently kicked his computer's base unit just beyond the tips of his outstretched fingers. Recoiling his arm, he stood up and pushed his oversized leather chair out of the way and assumed a position on all fours under the imitation cherry wood desk the district had given him to make him look authoritative.

Grabbing a hold of the large Hewlett Packard computer base, he slid it back into its proper location. As he reached out again with his right hand, his eyes caught a glimpse of a small object that looked vaguely familiar. Just below the system reset button was a small green light. Having just depressed the power button, he knew this light could not be an indicator of the computer still being turned on. This light resembled the one he had noticed and forgotten all about three weeks ago on the dash of his SUV. It was also identical to the light he had dismissed as nothing more than a dream that same night lying in bed.

Looking over his shoulder, he noticed the clock hanging on the wall next to his certificates displayed a time of 2:20. He still had thirty minutes until the kids were dismissed and he was expected to be outside helping them stay out of trouble, and correcting the few who couldn't help it.

It was against school board policy for anyone to perform maintenance on any property belonging to the district except a certified technician. Fully aware of the policy, James believed it would be acceptable to make an exception this once. He did not consider himself to be a technology wizard by any stretch of the imagination, but he knew he could unscrew the housing on his computer's tower and return it back to its rightful place in the half hour he had remaining and nobody would be the wiser. Not only did he feel he could do it; he felt he had to do it. Three weeks ago he had first witnessed the light in his SUV and had vowed to find its source. Having been disturbed by other thoughts each time he climbed into his automobile, he had forgotten all about it. This was the third such light in three weeks. Not thinking he would find anything like what he would soon discover, James let his curiosity overwhelm him and soon had four screws off of the unit with two to go.

With the housing for the computer base lying on the floor, James made a brief exploration of the unit's interior. He had no clue what all of the chips and wires did, nor did he have any idea what he was looking for, but thought nonetheless he would attempt to find out what was attached to the glowing light on the exterior of the plastic case. Thirty seconds into his search, he found what he was looking for.

Last November Christy had asked him to begin preparing Travis's baby room. Knowing she could go into labor at any moment, she wanted the peace of mind that if she were rushed off to the hospital her baby boy would have a beautiful room to welcome him when he made his first trip to his new home.

Christy did not trust her husband to make what she called, "reasonable decisions" about the room's décor, so he had been delegated to tasks of putting together all of the purchased furniture, installing the sound makers, and mounting the monitors. Christy had made it clear throughout the nine months of her pregnancy that she intended to spare no expense for their soon-to-be born son. This was evident to James as he worked on placing that contraption on the wall exactly twenty-four inches above the mattress located in Travis's crib.

According to Christy, the device James was installing was the newest and best variety of baby monitor on the market. As described on the packaging, this monitor could do it all. Not only could parents hear their kids cry from any room in the house, this monitor made it possible for parents to view their child sleeping in his crib from any room in the house at any time day or night.

The monitor was equipped with a small camera shaped similar to a tube of his wife's lipstick. It could supposedly capture the image of whatever was placed directly in front of it. Although the monitor showed the best resolution for objects between eighteen and thirty inches away, it was capable of observing objects as much as ten feet away. A small green bulb just above the lens provided just enough light for the camera to capture images in the darkest of night as well as provide an indication that the power to the unit was on.

Hunched under his desk with the computer's innards on display beside him on the floor, James was staring at a device remarkably familiar to the small camera tube mounted to the wall in his son's room. *Is this object a camera as well? If so is this one of those new web cams like those on display in the electronics stores?* He didn't think so. *If it is, why does this one have a light indicating that it is turned on?* He hadn't turned it on or installed it. Even more interestingly, why had he seen a similar light in his car and again on the picture frame in the sanctuary of his bedroom?

Chapter Seven

J ames hung up the phone unsatisfied after hearing a recorded message telling him that the technology department was closed and would not be available to offer assistance until the first week in July. Glancing at the clock, he noticed he had four minutes to reassemble the pile of plastic and silicone resting on the floor and get outside to supervise as the students celebrated the conclusion of another year.

As the last bus pulled away, James again found his mind drifting to the thought of the small green lights that seemed to be popping up everywhere he looked.

An hour later, he was sitting in his driver's seat reaching over the armrest that separated him from the place that Christy normally sat. Opening the glove compartment, he rifled through napkins that had been jammed in after the family's last dinner on-the-go and grabbed two small books. The one he held on top was the owner's manual given to him at the dealership describing all of the features in his new Chevy Blazer; the other, a pamphlet of directions for operating his upgraded stereo system.

Deciding to first flip open the automobile's owner's manual, he turned through all 164 pages in an attempt to find something referencing the small green light that was once again shining at him a foot and a half away. Finding nothing, he opened the second book. Aside from learning how to program another twenty stations on the preset buttons, James learned nothing new.

On the back page of the pamphlet, he located a 1-800 number that could be dialed by people in need of customer service. Picking up his cell phone and dialing the number, James shifted his transmission into drive and began his trip home. Ten minutes and seven miles later, he was speaking with a man from the maintenance and support department. After describing the tiny green light staring at him and articulating his questions to the twenty something computer geek on the other end, James was again left disappointed and this time a little angry. Not only was Stephen, the technology support representative, not able to answer any of his questions, James was also told that he must have been confused because no such light, or camera as he believed it to be, had ever been installed on any of their equipment.

Frustrated, James hung up the phone, looked up to see the light he was driving under turn to red, and said a silent prayer that he would not be mailed a ticket along with a photograph of himself breaking the law in plain view of the new cameras that had just been installed by the road commission to catch people doing exactly what he had just done.

Arriving home fifteen minutes later, he once again decided not to let the lights become another thing for his wife to tease him about. They had not caused him any harm. His mind was probably just getting carried away because of all of the talk he had heard on the news lately. He was sure they were nothing and refused to obsess about them.

Chapter Eight

Two weeks into his summer, James was already fully immersed into his new schedule. Going into his office on Mondays, Tuesdays, and Wednesdays at around nine in the morning and arriving back home at one o'clock, James was away from his wife and child for only twelve hours a week—a much better way to live than spending the fifty-five hours a week at school that he did the other nine months out of the year.

This morning, Christy opted to let James sleep in as she got up to her son's faint babblings sometime soon after the sun came up. The light shining through the blinds in his room always woke him up earlier than his parents hoped. Unluckily for them, during the summer in their part of the northern hemisphere, sunrise was sometime near 5:45.

It was nine thirty when James finally crawled out of bed. Walking down the stairs, he noticed Travis sitting on the floor surrounded by a mountain of primary colored plastic. For the first three months of his son's life, James was wondering if all of the money they had invested into the newest and best educational toys had been a wise investment. During those days, Travis had shown little interest in anything other than nursing and sleeping. Recently and suddenly that had all changed. It seemed now as if each day Travis had a different toy that took on the role as his favorite.

As he approached the bottom of the stairs, he noticed Christy, already showered and dressed in a pair of blue jeans and a sweater, sitting on a blanket about five feet from her little man.

"We're just trying to figure out what to keep and what to get rid of. The house is just getting way too cluttered with all of this stuff piling up. I thought I would pull everything out and let him decide what he gets to keep and what you get to store in the basement. I told him he could keep five things so he needed to choose wisely. I hope he understood. All he said back to me was booboo baba."

"Five? There are more than twenty things there now. Where exactly am I supposed to put the rest? Can't we just give them away or sell them?" James questioned while rubbing the sleep out of his eyes.

"James, you forget we will need this stuff for our future kids. If we get rid of this stuff now, we'll just have to go buy it all again later, and you know that whenever that is I'll have to go buy whatever the newest gadgets are. I won't be able to settle for the old when I'm out looking for the new. I'm sure you can find room downstairs somewhere, behind the TV, under the stairs, next to your tools. I know if you rearrange some of your belongings you will be able to make room for some of your only son's."

With a heavy sigh, James replied, "I'm sure I can. Are you just going to keep out the first five toys he touches?"

With a glance at her son and a gentle laugh she said, "Actually he has already picked five. These are all of the toys we are getting rid of. I just wanted him to have one last hoorah before you take them all downstairs."

Looking at the pile of Fisher Price, Disney, and Barney, James let out a deep breath before saying, "I'll get on it right after a cup of coffee."

Two hours later what used to be James's Man Room began to resemble an aisle at Babies-R-Us. Where he used to have his bobble head collection, he now had a Sesame Street stuffed animal. On top of his poker table he had a big yellow school bus. Two more trips to the living room and he would have everything out of Christy's way and into his.

Looking around at what used to be his domain, James realized that his life was never going to be the same. No longer could he grab a Coke, a bag of potato chips, and venture to his spot of isolation and watch whatever game ESPN had chosen to broadcast. With a son to take care of in addition to a wife to entertain, anytime he did decide to take a moment to himself, guilt would overwhelm him. How could he justify taking time to be all by himself when his wife spent every moment of the day raising his child?

With Travis in her arms, Christy came downstairs to check on the status of her husband. With an astonished look on her face she asked, "What happened down here? Where did your room go?"

"I had to rearrange some things in order to make room for my little guy to share The Man Room with me," James said with a quick smile.

"I'm glad you're ready to have another man in the house, but I think it's going to be a while before he is ready to sit down and analyze the NFL draft with you down here. Why didn't you just pile his stuff up under the stairs?" she said, pointing towards the dark storage space under the steps she had just descended.

"You may have to move some of those cans of paint the builder left behind, and you may need to knock down a few cobwebs, but I think you can probably fit everything under there and still be able to keep your little paradise."

Picking up the remote control and turning the TV on to another rerun of *Sportscenter,* James leaned in and gave Christy a peck on the cheek.

"Great idea babe. I'll go get a broom and start cleaning. I should have this done before the *Plays of the Week* are over."

Climbing into the small cavity where his wife had suggested he create a storage closet, James quickly decided this was not going to be enjoyable. Not only was he slightly claustrophobic, he also considered himself an arachnophobe. As he got down onto his hands and knees with a flashlight wedged between his teeth, he illuminated what appeared to be a small town of spiders, all congregated and waiting to make something their dinner. After just a few seconds, he was already beginning to feel like he was covered in the silky webs that had been strung from one corner of the opening to the other. He was in no mood for this.

Instead of taking his time and neatly piling up the toys in a position that would fully utilize the space, he grabbed a hold of each item and tossed them into the darkness. Five minutes later he was done and heading upstairs.

Chapter Nine

It was during the first week of August that James came to the realization that what had been an incredible summer was coming to an end. The kids were scheduled to report for class during the third week of the month. As a member of the office staff, his contract mandated that he arrive at least two weeks prior. This meant that he only had three days left to enjoy the company of his family before returning to the drama that comprised his career.

Usually at some point during the last couple of days of the summer, Christy took the time to create a honey-do list for her husband to complete before his final weekend off. As of Friday, he still hadn't received this note and he had no intention of asking about it. Maybe with all of the time Christy was spending with Travis she simply forgot. Whatever the reason, he planned on enjoying some peace and quiet. Unfortunately his plans came to an abrupt end as he entered the kitchen to retrieve his morning cup of coffee. Seated at the table was Christy who was feeding their son a jar of what looked like smashed pears. Next to her was a small pocket notebook, with an ink pen lying across the top. Under the pen was written a list, *the list*.

Walking to the table, he greeted his wife with a kiss and tore out the sheet of paper.

"What's this?" he asked, already knowing the disappointing truth.

"It's just a few things I was hoping you could do before you go back to work. I know you want to relax as much as possible, but these jobs should all be really quick. I'm even taking Travis to a play date today if you want to get it all done then."

"This doesn't look too bad. I'll get it done," he replied walking out of the room.

The list was shorter than usual. After reading all that his wife wanted him to do, his confidence in having a restful weekend came back. Aside from mowing the lawn and sweeping the garage, which were his weekly chores anyway, there was only one more task for him to complete; carry the Exersaucer that their son had outgrown down to the basement to be placed with all of the spiders under the stairs. He would do that first and then spend a couple of hours outside finishing up before hopefully spending the rest of the day watching something mind-numbing on the TV.

Down in the basement and once again on his hands and knees, James held the attachment in his hands that would allow him to suck dozens of spiders and webs into the canister of a portable shop vac. Ridding the storage space of these sources of fear gave him more confidence to crawl in and rearrange the existing boxes and stuffed animals to make room for the larger box he had brought down from upstairs containing, what he believed, should be just another garage sale item. Regardless of what she told him, Christy would not want to recycle these toys for a future child. She would want to buy everything brand new whenever they were lucky enough to have another kid.

Lying the flashlight on the floor, he tried to shift his pile of cardboard from the entrance into a spot deeper into the cave he had discovered under the stairs. Shifting his weight to make himself more comfortable, James accidentally kicked the light he had set by his right knee so that the beam began to shine on the wall at the back of the space. Following the height of the staircase, the wall rose to a height of about ten feet. Reaching to grab the light to redirect it back to his work, he noticed the object he had been looking to discover for months without even realizing it.

Rising to a crouch, James reached up towards the spot where the flashlight was causing the brightest reflection. There, while in his stooped position, at eye level was what appeared to be a doorknob. A knob unlike the silver latches placed on every other door in the house. This knob was a standard brass knob similar to those that were in his and Christy's first small starter home—a fifty-year-old ranch located about twenty miles from their current home.

Thinking back to when he and his wife sat down with the contractor to go over the blueprints for this house, he did not remember seeing any plans for an extra closet to be placed in such a dark place. Perhaps this was just a doorway into another crawlspace where he could store more stuff.

Brushing aside a web he must have missed with the vacuum, he grabbed a hold of the round knob and turned. It moved easily, but the same was not true of the door it was attached to. Pushing forward with his shoulder, the door nudged open slightly and then swung all the way open causing him to land with his cheek flat on the floor.

Opening his eyes to the soft glow emanating from

somewhere near by, he was not prepared for what he saw lining the walls around him.

Chapter Ten

Upstairs Christy was just getting home from her morning with friends and their kids. Walking up to place her sleeping son in his crib, she realized that her husband was not where she expected to see him, sitting in his recliner with the remote in his hand. He must have been in the basement enjoying some freedom, she thought. On his last Friday off, she did not want to disturb him so she left him alone. After gently laying Travis down, she went to the kitchen to make some lunch. Sitting on the couch in the living room, she turned on the TV and began to watch one of the soap operas she had found herself addicted to since her son took on his latest nap schedule in the middle of the day.

Two hours after placing him to bed, Travis began to wake up. Christy could hear his faint babblings as he practiced one of the newest sounds he was able to articulate with his voice. Today it sounded as if he were making "D" sounds that almost resembled the word *Dada*. She contemplated the idea of going to get James so that he could enjoy this and revel in the idea that his son's first words may have been directed towards him, but decided against it. The closer she got to her son's room, the clearer his voice became. He was no longer babbling, but turning his sounds into a higher pitched cry. Apparently he was beginning to get over the "individual play time" his mom gave him for fifteen minutes after every nap and was ready to get out.

At four thirty that afternoon, Christy's patience with James was beginning to run out. He had given her his word that all of his chores would get done that day. She had even arranged a morning away from the house so that he could have some time to get them all done. Looking out the window in their small dining room, she could see that the lawn hadn't been touched. She walked over to the laundry room and opened the door that led into the garage and noticed the same piles of dirt and debris lying on the floor that had been there when she left in the morning. She had noticed that the Exersaucer had been removed from the living room, but she couldn't guarantee that James had actually found a place to store it. It was her belief that he grabbed the box, went downstairs, turned on the TV, and then got lost in his own world, probably taking a nap on his old fluffy recliner forgetting about the world around him.

She walked to the edge of the basement stairs and heard the sound she expected to hear, the dull hum of voices. She could see the flickering glow of the screen filling in the dark spaces ten feet below to confirm that the TV was on. Not wanting to walk all the way down with Travis in her arms, she called for her husband from where she was. The first two times she said his name she got no response, the third time she heard the panic in her husbands voice as he said, "Oh, um I...I'll be right there."

Two minutes later, a flush faced James was standing in front of his wife with a blank stare on his face.

"What were you doing down there? You promised that you were going to complete my list today. I've had Travis all day and you've just been hanging out downstairs," Christy said, while handing Travis off to James.

"I uh, just got a little distracted. I'll get on it right now," he said without further explanation. He sat his son down on the floor, gave him a toy truck to roll around and walked off to the garage.

Ten minutes later he found himself in the front yard pushing his lawn mower around. He was not taking the time to create diagonal lines like he normally did when manicuring the grass; instead he was virtually walking around aimlessly. He could not concentrate on the task at hand. He was too busy trying to figure out what he had stumbled into while trying to get some work done in the basement.

His initial thought of having discovered another crawl space to store paint and miscellaneous supplies had been quickly proven inaccurate as he crashed through the door about four hours ago. Instead of finding a musty room cluttered with old rags, paintbrushes, and rollers, he discovered a room that rivaled any other room in the upper two levels of his house for magnificence. The room was not crawling with spiders and critters looking for a safe place to call home, but was lined with shelves polished to a mirror like shine. Brass shelves covered every inch of wall space in the room and every inch of shelf space was occupied. There were film reels similar to the ones he had watched when growing up at his grandparents' house showing old family movies. There were small tapes with the word *Beta* written on them, VHS tapes and small cases containing DVDs. On the shelf directly across from the doorway he had entered was a large thirty or forty inch TV that appeared to be showing a movie, a movie that looked eerily familiar.

During his first few minutes in the room, James spent his time simply trying to rub out the bruises he earned when he fell through the door. Looking around, his initial thought was that he must have hit his head. Standing to his feet, he reached out and touched the shelf containing the DVDs and realized this was no dream or hallucination. This was a real place.

Looking at the monitor in front of him, he scrutinized the images flashing before him to try and figure out why this movie looked so familiar. He had seen this, or something like this somewhere before. He was witnessing a scene from what looked like a twenty year old film. The boys running around were all wearing shorts that even by today's standard would be considered risqué. At his school, girls were often sent home for wearing shorts that did not cover enough of their legs to fit into the dress code, but it had been a long time since he remembered boys wearing anything that short. Boys in this age were wearing shorts that were anything but. They were often so long that they covered their knees and sometimes even went down to their shins. He remembered when he was a little kid running around in true shorts, but that had been at least two decades ago.

The image showed kids climbing on a set of monkey bars at a park. It was a sunny day and the kids were all screaming and yelling. One boy in particular took up the majority of the screen. He was a heavy-set child wearing a sweat suit. Seeping from the corners of his shirt where the sleeves met his torso were dark sweat stains. His hair was disheveled and the braces attached to his top row of teeth could be seen glistening in the sun. It was upon seeing this kid that he recognized the scene.

He had been nine years old. He and his best friend Tommy had been virtually attached at the hip. During the summer, they spent each day together and often alternated spending nights in each other's houses. Jimmy was a skinny kid then and his best bud was the opposite. Together they found they formed a pretty impressive team. When they played football against other kids from the neighborhood, Tommy would be a great blocker allowing Jimmy to race by the opponents and score touchdown after touchdown. In his driveway at home, Jimmy would often invite other kids to challenge him and Tommy in basketball games. Tommy was a force down low and Jimmy was a superb outside shooter.

The day being played out in front of him was the day that had changed all of that. The boys had been best friends since being enrolled in kindergarten together. The day on the monkey bars had been the last time he had ever really talked to Tommy. By the time he entered high school he had all but forgotten his former blocking buddy.

As he remembered it, that day the boys had been playing with a large group of kids from the neighborhood. While playing, one child, whose name James could not remember, started making fun of Tommy for wearing his sweat suit on such a hot summer day. He couldn't remember the exact words that had been spoken, but he did remember that he did not defend his friend. Normally he would have spoken up and come to the aide of his buddy, but the kid that had been making fun of him that day was the most popular kid in school, a tall skinny fifth grader that all of the girls had a crush on. Not being able to remember his full name, James did know it was Kyle something. While observing all of this, James, as he remembered it, chose to just continue playing and kept his thoughts to himself.

What he was seeing on the TV, however, did not fit into what he remembered. On the screen he was seeing an image that brought him quite a bit of shame. He was able to see his friend Tommy struggling to make it all the way across the horizontal ladder separating the swings from the slide. His friend appeared to be stuck halfway. In the background he heard a voice. A child was yelling, "Tubby Tommy, Tubby Tommy." Looking from face to face, his former friend locked eyes with another small child. It couldn't be.

But it had to be. Wearing his old favorite neon orange shirt was a nine-year-old version of him, little Jimmy Carlise.

He could remember how he felt after the incident. He knew he had been a coward, and he knew that he had let his friend down. He had not done anything blatant, but he did not come to the aid of his friend. He did not remember making eye contact with Tommy at that moment, but apparently he had. He thought he had just blended in with the surroundings and merged in, but Tommy had seen him. He watched him turn his back on him when he needed him. He watched as Jimmy joined up with a newer, cooler group that would comprise his peer group through high school. He watched as Jimmy failed to turn around and even offer a customary "I'm sorry" glance at his despairing friend.

The scene faded from the monitor in front of him and

faded into another, and then another. In all, James relived fifteen moments from his childhood that he wished he could have forgotten. From the day he cheated on his physics final his junior year to the day he bumped fenders with a parked car at the mall, Jimmy was witness to events that he thought nobody knew about. He had not gotten into trouble for any of the things he was watching on the screen because he hadn't told anybody what he had done. *How in the world could anyone have captured all of these events on video?* When his son was born, he told himself that he would not allow Travis to make the same mistakes that he had made, but he did not want his son to know all of the bad decisions he had made during his childhood either. He had to find out who taped all of this stuff and figure out a way to hide it.

Taking his eyes off of the screen and looking at all of the shelves around him, he was filled with a sense of wonder. Was it possible that these were all movies of him? It wasn't likely. The thousands of videos contained in that room would account for virtually every minute of his life. Maybe this was some sort of video library his wife had created highlighting moments from both of their lives. If that were the case though, how did she acquire footage from before they even met? Beyond that, how had anyone captured these moments that he thought had taken place with so much secrecy?

In the background of his thoughts, he thought he heard someone calling his name. Backing up towards the entrance to the mysterious room, he was able to identify the voice of his wife calling his name. Shouting back that he would be right there, he quickly exited the room, crawled out of the storage space and climbed the stairs.

As he made another pass across his yard, he noticed the perspiration dripping off of his face. He was not sure what he had stumbled into down in the basement, but he wanted to find out. He would talk to Christy about it as soon as he got the chance.

Coming back into the house two hours later after completing his list of chores, he instantly began looking for Christy. He knew he had to talk to her about his discovery. *If she had compiled the inventory, why has she not told me about it? Why do I keep asking myself whether she knows anything about it? Of course she does! If I didn't put the movies together, nobody else could have possibly gained access to the room in the basement to store everything I have found but her.*

Hearing his wife upstairs, he began to climb the steps two at a time. Reaching the top, he discovered that his wife was already in The Jungle Room with Travis getting him ready for bed. James had been instructed numerous times to stay quiet at that time of the evening. Even the smallest sound would cause his son to stop whatever he was doing and begin looking around until he discovered the source. He had learned this lesson the hard way. When Travis was only a couple of weeks old, James decided that allowing his wife to spend all of that great quality time with their son each night while she fed and dressed him alone was not fair. He wanted to enjoy it as well. One night he stalked into the room while Christy was cuddling their son. With the light off it was very difficult to see, so James had to rely on his memory of the room's surroundings. Earlier in the day, apparently Christy had done some redecorating because as he high-stepped his way across the room his right foot stepped on what he discovered later was a giant teddy bear. Stepping on the bear did not cause any noise, but the whisper of profanity he had mumbled while asking what he stepped on had caused Travis to instantly stop what he was doing and look around. Forty-five minutes later, Christy was finally able to get Travis back on schedule, but not before whispering to her husband to never enter the room again while she was feeding or getting Travis ready for bed.

For that reason, James decided he would wait for Christy to come out of the room before beginning his discussion. To kill the time, he walked down the hall to his small office and turned on his computer to check his e-mail.

Scrolling through a seemingly endless list of junk mail, his mind again began to drift to the library of videos he had discovered in the basement. While visualizing the vastness of the surroundings, he was forced to ask himself yet another question. How in the world did Christy pay for all of that without his knowledge? Last year when he discussed the idea of getting the family a new TV for a Christmas present, Christy had told him that they could not afford it. They were not exactly living paycheck to paycheck, but they were trying to pay off all of their debt. James had accumulated quite a bit of financial aid that the couple was determined to pay back as quickly as possible. There was no way that his wife would have purchased anything on their credit card. They had agreed to only use their Visa in an emergency. The items that had been placed downstairs were easily worth thousands of dollars. It was true that he allowed his wife to handle all of the family's finances, but there was no way she could have hidden such an investment.

It was true that she could have used some of her time at home during the day to set everything up and move it into the room, but if she had wanted it to be some sort of secret, why would she have recommended that he place all of the baby toys in such a close proximity. She had to have known he would see it.

If this were supposed to be some sort of surprise, would he ruin it by telling her what he had found? He knew how much pride his wife took every year on his birthday to provide him with the perfect present. Perhaps this was preparation for his next birthday in October. Maybe she thought with all of the spiders that surrounded the area, James would be content to throw the toys under the stairs and not really climb under and would therefore never find the room.

Maybe it would be better to remain silent on the subject just a little longer. If she wanted or expected him to find the room while doing the list, he was sure she would ask him about it. If it were to be some sort of secret, it was definitely in his best interest to act ignorant of the subject. He would wait until the next time Christy left the house and he would check it out again. Until then he would just wait and see if she had anything to say to him about it.

Chapter Eleven

During the first week that James was back to work, he found himself often daydreaming about the mysterious room he had discovered just before his final weekend of vacation. Christy had not let on that she knew anything about it, and he had not been given anytime alone to do more investigating. Luckily for him, the kids at school were keeping him busy and allowing him to think about other things for most of the day. Each evening, however, as he pulled up the driveway, he found himself hoping that Christy would not be in the house. He just needed a few minutes to explore without being interrupted or being found out. He did not want his wife to know that he had discovered what was down there in the recesses under the stairs until he could figure out exactly what it was.

Sitting down for dinner on Thursday, Christy brought up a topic that immediately captured his attention. With Travis eating some sort of finger food in his high chair, James and his wife were able to enjoy some time sitting near each other discussing the day's events. James told her how he suspended three kids who had attempted a food fight and about the parent who had already come in asking for a schedule change for her son, because she knew there would be too many personality conflicts between her son and the teachers he was currently assigned to. Christy explained that nothing dramatic had happened in her day, but that she did call up her cousin Kelly to RSVP for the baby shower she was hosting on Saturday. She explained that she would be bringing Travis to show him off a little bit, but she promised not to be gone long, a couple of hours maximum.

Trying his best not to act too excited, James nonchalantly shrugged his shoulders and said, "Sounds like fun. Don't feel like you have to rush home. You deserve some time out. Have a good time."

Laughing to herself Christy smiled and said, "A baby shower is not necessarily a night on the town, but thanks. The party starts at noon so we'll leave around eleven thirty and be back by two. I'm sure you'll be able to find a game or something to keep you busy."

"Yeah, I'll probably just hang out in the basement and spend some time in The Man Room."

Chapter Twelve

Kissing his son and wife goodbye on Saturday morning, James walked to the living room where he could watch the Blazer pull out of the driveway. As the car rounded the first corner he went to the kitchen to grab the cordless phone normally stored on the counter next to the stove so that he could take it with him and answer it when his wife called to say she was on her way home. He then headed down to the basement to begin his investigation.

Swatting away the new cobwebs that had formed in the last week, he assumed a position on his hands and knees and crawled for the door he had found eight days earlier. Reaching up and grabbing a hold of the doorknob, he gave a hard shove and again fell to the floor inside the doorway to the room he had been waiting a week to revisit.

The first place his eyes focused on was the monitor displaying a movie much different than the ones he had viewed a week prior. The visual quality of the images was very scratchy. The characters seemed to almost move as robots with herky-jerky spasms. There was no sound, but he could tell the people were speaking because their mouths were moving. The scene was a beach. The people were all dressed in bathing suits that to him looked very outdated. The women wore one piece suits most of which were accompanied by ruffles around the waist resembling skirts. He remembered his mom used to dress like that whenever she took him to the city pool. He believed, as a mom she was trying to be modest, or perhaps she just lacked the confidence in herself to wear the types of suits that many of the younger girls were wearing. The men were all wearing bathing suits that by today's standards would be considered *Speedos*. Not quite bikini bottoms, but still awfully short.

As the cameraman made a sweep of the beach, families could be seen having picnics. Kids were building sand castles, and women were trying to gather suntans. In the distance, James noticed a water tower with the words *Pensacola Beach* scrawled across. He had been to that beach. When he was young, before even attending kindergarten, his parents had taken him for what was to be a fun-filled vacation. He didn't remember much about the trip, but he knew it was that vacation that helped him acquire his fear of water. Growing up, his parents had told him that they were given information about the Gulf Coast of Florida and were told it was a perfect place to take a family. James' dad had been in the military for a few years prior to getting married and settling down with his family. Buddies of his had been sent to Pensacola for Officer Training and had bragged about how great the scenery was. The beaches were beautiful and the water was calm the guys had told him. This was the first vacation James remembered taking with the whole family and the one that stuck with him the most because although everyone else still described the trip as one of rest and relaxation, he remembered it differently.

As he continued to watch the movie, he saw that the

videographer was beginning to zoom in on something happening in the water. About twenty feet off the shore, groups of teenagers were gathered on a shallow sandbar, but this was not what the cameraman was trying to capture. Instead, he was narrowing in on a small boy wading in the water. The kid, who was probably not even old enough to be enrolled in school, was moving towards the older kids gathered throwing around a football in ankle deep water, but in his case the water was already up near his chest. As he continued to move out towards the sandbar, the water continued to rise on his body until all at once he was gone from view.

It was at that moment that James realized what he was watching. When he was four years old on his family trip to the beach, he attempted to go out into the water and play with the big kids. He had not taken a swim lesson at any point in his life, and had never had a desire to swim anywhere but the baby pool at his city's local park. That day at the beach, he had inadvertently stepped off an embankment hidden under the rolling waves as they came to shore. As he stepped off the slope, the water instantaneously rose over his head and panic set in. Instead of trying to jump up and signal for help, he found himself opening his mouth and swallowing huge amounts of seawater.

Later on, his parents told him that he had been a very lucky boy. He was not supposed to have gone in the water by himself, as it was not safe. They believed that somehow a large wave had found its way over the barrier of the sandbar and had washed him back to shore just in time. It wasn't until one of the other moms on the beach noticed him laying face down in the shallow surf and screamed that his parents had even noticed that he was missing. After being dragged back up onto the sand, he somehow was able to regain consciousness and then, through tears, tell his mom that he hated the water and that he would never go swimming again.

With the exception of showering and an occasional rest in a hot tub, that was a vow he had kept throughout his life. Each time his family went to the pool or to the beach, he packed a book and a towel and spent his time dry, watching the others have their version of fun. It was that decision that had probably given him such a love for reading. From choose-your-own adventure stories to American classics, he had spent his summers engrossed in novels while his family splashed away.

Continuing to watch the video screen before him, James began to second-guess his earlier estimation of what he was viewing. This couldn't be another home movie of him. Not only did his family not own a camera until he was a teenager, his parents had told him numerous times that they did not see him go into the water. Whoever was taping this scene seemed to know what was going to happen. Instead of recording all of the action on the sandbar, this person had chosen to focus on the small boy wading through the water.

As he watched the boy walk deeper and deeper into the ocean, he noticed something else that contrasted from his own memory. In his situation, he remembered entering the water alone. He was not escorted by any adult and that had been the reason he had almost drowned. The young boy in this video, however, was being escorted by a man resembling someone straight out of Woodstock. The boy was not talking to the man and even seemed to be ignoring him, so James doubted that the two were relatives or even acquaintances. The older man, probably in his thirties, looked out of place. He had a long beard, long hair, and what appeared to be a T-shirt purchased three sizes too large because it hung off of him like a dress.

As he continued to watch, James got an uncomfortable feeling. He noticed that although the young boy in the video did not appear to even notice the older man, the same could not be said of the hippie. He was in fact very aware of the little sandy haired kid. He was not talking to him, but staring at him. He was walking about five feet behind the child and James began to feel even more unsettled.

What was he watching? He had heard about scenes like this on the radio and had seen reenactments on shows like America's Most Wanted. Why was this in his basement? Although he thought he knew what he was about to see, James could not take his eyes away from the screen. Watching as the boy took a few more steps, he saw him quickly get swallowed up by the surface of the water and disappear. Taking two long strides, the man in the dress was standing in what appeared to be the same spot that the boy had just been. He watched as the man reached both of his hands below the waves, James cringed as he thought about the man trapping the child under the surface. *How could anyone be so twisted as to hurt a child, especially when he was as vulnerable as this one was?* Turning away from the screen for a split second, James missed the moment he had been anticipating; however, as he could see from the screen, that moment had obviously not happened. The little boy had not been held under the water because he was now lying up on the shore.

Just before the screen switched to a static snowstorm, James again was forced into an unsettled feeling. Standing above the child as he lay there crying and coughing up water was a woman wearing a large pair of sunglasses that made her look like a grasshopper standing on two legs. At least that was what he had told his mom she looked like when she wore glasses just like that.

Chapter Thirteen

Resting under the white down comforter his wife had purchased for their bed, James looked at the clock by his head for the tenth time in just as many minutes. Two thirty, and the little red light was still shining in the corner. Next to it, James could also see the glowing green bulb, he had almost forgotten about, situated on top of the framed picture of him and his wife. He couldn't sleep. All he could do was think about what he had discovered that afternoon, and now he was seeing those strange lights again. Were they somehow related? Was he just imagining things? Was the stress of trying to have a family, a career, and privacy getting to him? It couldn't all just be his imagination. It's not like he was just seeing things. He was able to hear things on the monitor downstairs. He was able to run his fingers over the smooth polished shelves holding all of the videos in the room. If he was having some sort of breakdown, it just didn't make sense that he would be able to experience everything in such a real way...but maybe that is what every crazy person thinks just before they lose it.

Earlier in the day after the monitor showed him the movie that had somehow been taken of him on his family vacation and then somehow had been edited to include additional characters that were not in the real life scene that he remembered, James had tuned his gaze to the shelves that lined the walls of the room. Covering every inch of the space were videos. The spine of each tape and DVD contained a variety of images and these images were what had kept him awake all night.

Looking around the room at first he saw what he believed were volumes of cases containing the same things, but as he looked closer he noticed that indeed there were some differences. The videos placed along the wall to his right all had an identifying mark on the bottom edge resembling a smiling face. The videos on the left wall all contained a crying face, while the videos on the wall behind him contained a small cartoon of a face with no mouth or expression at all. Surrounding the large TV screen on the front wall were piles of DVDs all identified with dates stamped onto the bottom edge. The dates however did not indicate when the movies had been taken, as he was to discover, but instead they indicated dates to come, beginning with the following day and continuing on for at least the next forty years.

Picking up the square case containing the next day's date he was surprised to see that it was still sealed in a transparent plastic wrap similar to those found on CDs at his favorite music store in the mall. He had rifled through a few of the piles hoping to find the disc that contained that day's date, but had not been able to before his curiosity led him to the shelf on his left.

Reaching out with his right hand, he grabbed a hold of the largest case he could see. Pulling it off the shelf, he almost dropped the container that had weighed as much as a phone book. Bracing it with his left hand, he flipped it over to see if anything was written on the top of the box. Discovering another small picture of a crying face, he also noticed the words *Freshman Year* inscribed across the top two inches.

Placing the box on the floor, he proceeded to lift the lid off of it to discover what was inside. As he pulled the lid up he was able to see a small mountain of what looked like miniature tapes similar to the ones he used with his personal video camera. He was able to pick up the top one just before he heard the noise that had caused him to switch into scurry mode. Above him he was able to hear the footsteps of his wife walking around the first floor, probably looking for him. Throwing the tape back into its box he paused as he noticed the date written in gold lettering along its face. It was exactly fourteen years ago, the same date as when he moved into his dorm room at Northern State University.

His first two years of college were marred with ups and downs. He came to the school without knowing a soul. In high school he had always been popular and able to make friends so he wasn't worried about moving in blind with three other guys into his two hundred square foot dorm room. He actually looked forward to making a new batch of best friends. He remembered move-in day.

Walking into the tall eight-story building alone, he glanced around at all of the other freshmen carrying their most valuable possessions in garbage bags while moms and dads cried and held hands. His parents were not able to make the trip from out of state, but his dad had accompanied him to the orientation that had taken place the previous month. On move-in day, however, he was forced to carry everything up to the fifth floor by himself. Of all of the days for the elevators to be broken that day was the worst. Luckily for him all of his belongings fit into one large sea bag, so he would not have to climb up and down more than once.

By the time he made it to his room all of his roommates had already arrived. One was a member of the school's soccer team; one had already attained a job acting as a DJ for a local club, and the other was a self-proclaimed future Gold Glove boxer. The four eighteen-year-olds all made quick introductions discussing whether they were single or dating, where they were from, sports played, and other trivial biographical data. After no more than ten minutes the guys knew all about each other and decided it was time to christen their newfound friendship. Mike, the slim welterweight, walked to his mini-fridge and opened the door. Reaching inside, he grabbed four beers and passed them out to each of the guys. James was not about to admit that he was not a drinker. Aside from his time discussing student council activities in high school, he had never drank before. That moment, however, while trying to impress the guys he would spend the next four years with, changed him. His inability to take a stand and be honest with himself and others led him to a college career spent constantly working to attain the respect of his peers.

Looking back, he knew he had done a lot of partying that first year, but could not remember all of the details behind his nights out. He often forgot most of the events from the previous night by the time he woke up the next morning feeling dehydrated and having a pounding headache. In high school, he had always been one of the good guys. Sure he had been a goof off at times and had used his popularity to his own advantage, but he had never done anything that he felt truly compromised his future or his safety. Even his fling with Sam had been justified by his heart. He believed that if something felt good and you did not feel guilty about experiencing joy from an activity, it couldn't be that bad. Sam had definitely brought him joy, and instead of making him feel guilty, he had been granted great stories to share with his friends, and sometimes even complete strangers. Many times during his freshman year, however, things had been different. The nights out, the drinking, the socializing with girls was often taxing on his mind and body and only brought him temporary pleasure, not to mention the moments spent the next morning lying in bed had him asking himself, "Why did I do that?" Sometimes the guilt was so deep he even made promises to himself that were always broken, swearing to never do that again.

Climbing the stairs at home to greet his wife, James found himself making a similar promise to himself. The room he had discovered was causing him to think of a lot of questions. Each time he went down there, he was forced to remember something from his past that he no longer wanted to think about. It wasn't quite guilt that he was feeling for his past, but regret. Each step he climbed brought him closer to seeing his reason for living, his wife and child. He often spoke with Christy about how different their lives would have been if they had each done just a couple of things a little bit differently. James shuddered as he thought about his past and what it could have meant for his future. At that moment, he vowed not to return to the secret room until he was able to acquire some real answers.

Lying in bed, he contemplated the questions that needed answering. *What am I looking at down there? How had someone been able to tape all of these moments without my knowledge? Why had someone taped all of these moments in the first place? Are the tiny green lights that are popping up from time to time somehow connected? Could they actually be cameras placed strategically to spy on me?* Without answers to these questions, James would not return to his past or whatever else was hidden beneath the floor he so often stood on. With a deep sigh signifying his conviction to give up trying to find satisfactory answers, James rolled over, kissed his wife on the shoulder and closed his eyes.

Chapter Fourteen

As the days turned to weeks, James found he could not shake the mystery room from his mind. He was no closer to discovering who had placed all of those moments in his basement or why they were there. When he had made the vow to avoid returning to his secret chamber, he had intended to either discover the answers to his many questions or to at least put it out of his mind so that he could focus on his present life. So far, he had been able to do neither.

The week leading up to Halloween was always one of dread as he found himself engaged in seemingly endless battles with students and parents about why children twelve years old could not dress up as vampires, pirates, cowboys, and a number of other characters popular in that given year. He was always amazed that people could not understand how fake swords, guns, and blood dripping fangs could pose a distraction to the learning environment of others. That was his standard quote to parents almost regardless of the offense caused by their children. It was his job "to uphold the integrity of the learning environment." He hated getting into arguments with adults in front of kids, so he would always resort to that line when he felt a debate brewing. That excuse had just come into play as he explained to Mrs. Jamison, one of his frequent office visitors, that her son Dominic would be suspended for three days as a result of his decision to dress up as a demonic monster fully cloaked in spikes, chains, and a bloody hatchet.

Mom believed that Dommy was just a kid that loved to play make believe. Dommy had always had an active imagination and was a good boy. In her words, "He would never purposefully set out to violate any school rules." It didn't matter to her that Mr. Carlise had gotten on the morning announcements just the day before to remind students about appropriate dress and behavior during that week, because, after all, he probably couldn't hear the announcements that morning because of all of the other kids that were talking during his first hour. He had come home numerous times in the past, after all, and complained about the teachers who were constantly targeting her son while it was always the kids sitting next to him that were the real problem.

After an exhausting fifteen minutes, James finally told Mrs. Jamison that he had another meeting that he was late for, so he would have to cut the discussion short. Unfortunately her son had made a decision that had distracted the learning environment of others and he would have to pay the consequence. If she disagreed with his decision she was welcome to contact the school board and explain her position to them, which she loudly promised to do.

After walking her out of his office, James heard his secretary, Betty, let out a small snicker as he turned around and took a deep breath and rolled his eyes in an aggravated arch. Closing his door, James plopped into his swivel chair and began to list a number of expletives in his mind to describe the ignorance of the parent he had just met with. This type of activity was necessary for him from time to time. After all, some people were just so ridiculous. As long as he didn't verbalize his thoughts he believed he was doing nothing wrong.

Although his building was a nightmare to work in during the final week of October, his district had given him a small reward. With Halloween falling on a Friday, the school board had made the decision that everyone would be much better served by providing a three-day weekend. The students would just be too squirrelly on Friday and teachers would be spending their entire day providing discipline, so as a result Thursday would serve as the final day in what felt like the year's longest work week, although it was actually one of the shortest.

Walking through the door of his house at about five thirty Thursday afternoon, James jokingly announced as he always did, "The man of the house is home." Responding by meeting him by the kitchen table and offering a small kiss on the cheek, Christy could see how exhausted her husband was simply by looking at the bags under his eyes and the slow way in which he placed his briefcase on the floor.

"Why don't you go down to the basement and relax for a little while? I'll bring you down some dinner and a Coke. You can just watch some TV and unwind for a little while. You deserve it. Travis is taking a nap right now anyway. I'll just come get you when he wakes up."

Christy was great. She knew exactly how to bring new life into her husband. Looking up at his wife, James adjusted the look on his face to display a smile and said, "Thanks hon. I appreciate it. I promise I'll give you all day tomorrow to do whatever you want."

Taking off his jacket as he walked, James turned around the

corner separating his kitchen from the living room and made a b-line for the basement stairs. After grabbing the remote control and turning on his TV, James found himself snuggling into the recliner that seemed to be custom made for him. To a stranger, the chair would have looked like a lumpy seat destined for The Salvation Army, but after sitting in that chair almost every single day since before he was married, the cushions had formed themselves to the contours of his body.

The TV was tuned to one of the stations that showed old football and basketball games that someone now titled classics. The game he was watching had to have been at least forty years old, because he did not recognize a single player on either team. Just before turning the channel, he noticed something on the screen that diverted his attention. The game being shown was being broadcast in black and white. In the poor lighting that was installed in his basement it was difficult to actually focus on the action taking place inside the screen. What his eyes more naturally focused on were the reflections being cast off of the glass screen by objects around the room. As he looked to the top right corner of the screen where the score was being displayed, James was able to make out the reflection for the small cubby located under the stairs he had climbed down just a few minutes prior.

A year ago he would have been able to quickly adjust his eyes and focus on the telecast. This year, however, things were different. He knew that hidden behind those stairs was a secret he had been trying to figure out for months. He hadn't been back there for a couple of weeks, but he hadn't stopped thinking about it. He had promised himself not to return until he was able to figure out exactly what was going on with everything he had discovered. After eight weeks of dead ends, he didn't know what else to do. He had subtly mentioned to Christy how much he wished he had home movies from his childhood to share with Travis, hoping to get some sort of reaction from her. She had none. Normally she was a woman who was very easy to read. Every year at Christmas she begged him to let her give him at least one present early. If she had been responsible for all of those tapes, he was sure she would have responded with more energy than she had.

He had called all of the companies with which he had owned credit cards in the past ten years to see if there had been any purchases made that might explain for the high tech equipment that accompanied all of the tapes, reels, and discs only to turn up nothing.

As he sat there staring at the reflection bouncing off of his TV, James knew he was now being confronted by the need to make a decision. He had promised himself not to return without answers, but now he wondered if he would ever get the answers. If he did return to The Room, as he now referred to it in his mind, he would have to do so quickly because Christy could come downstairs with his dinner and/or his son at anytime.

Giving into his sense of curiosity and releasing himself of any guilt for going back on his promise, he got up and scurried to the hidden door. Leaning against it while turning the knob, James rocked his body backwards and then sharply struck the door with his shoulder giving him access to the mysteries within.

Once again he was greeted by not only four walls lined with an assortment of recordings, but images already being broadcast on the monitor hung on the center of the wall in front of him. The images on display this time did not seem to be as old as the others he had seen. This time he was watching a scene that looked very familiar, yet not quite.

In the center of the screen was a picture of himself sitting behind his desk at work. He had his eyes closed and appeared to be thinking, then his mouth opened and he looked up. Standing in front of him was a middle-aged man with long hair and a beard. James could hear himself in the movie mumbling something he could not quite understand, then all of a sudden he was able to make out the words spewing from his mouth, only these were words he couldn't ever remember articulating aloud. The James on the screen was yelling at the tall longhaired man. He was pouring forth obscenities and calling him a despicable adult and a worthless parent.

He knew he had never spoken like that to anyone. If he had, he wouldn't have been able to hold onto his job for as long as he had. Parents were always running to the school board to complain about injustices. If he had spoken to that man in that way he could guarantee that the board would have found out about it. Even if that man had not reported him, with the level at which he was yelling, every person in the main office would have heard him and he knew one of them would have discussed this event with him.

How anyone had been able to doctor this footage to make him look so disparaging was beyond him and even a little frightening. If anyone other than himself ever saw it, he would definitely have some questions to answer. The only thing he had going for him was that he knew the events being depicted were completely false. As long as that tape never made it out into the public, he would have nothing to worry about. He did have a few concerns, however. He wondered if there were more copies of the tape. And for something so obviously fictionalized, why did the scene look so familiar? Was it just because he was the main character and the setting was the office he had worked in for so many years? Why did that man with the beard look familiar? He didn't think he was the parent of any kid at his school, but he was pretty sure he had seen him before.

While trying to make sense of what he was witnessing, James was startled back to the present by the sudden sound of a door squeaking upstairs. The hinges on the door leading to the basement had been in need of a WD-40 squirt for a few weeks now and he just kept forgetting. Now he was grateful for that fact. The squeak had served as a doorbell to notify him that Christy was on her way down to see him. Two quick steps brought James through the door and into the cubby under the stairs. Hearing his wife directly above him, James darted out of the small opening just as Christy's left foot lifted off of the bottom stair. Bending over and pretending to smash a spider, James looked up and displayed a startled look to his smiling wife who held in her arms a plate covered with French fries and a homemade cheeseburger. Walking over to her, he offered his sincere thanks for bringing the warm meal to him, and returned to her the small kiss on the cheek she had greeted him with fifteen minutes prior. Blushing slightly, she told him it was no big deal and that she would head back upstairs and give him some more time to unwind by himself.

As she walked away, he thought to himself that he was very lucky to have such a great wife and family. It was at that moment that he realized why the movie he had watched in the secret room had looked so familiar. Earlier in the day after meeting with Mrs. Jamison, he had thought all of the things that the Mr. Carlise from the video had articulated. He hadn't said any of that stuff out loud though, and there definitely hadn't been anyone else in the room when he said it. The words that had been said, however, were the same words he had thought about saying.

Setting his plate down on his TV tray, James rushed back under the stairs hoping to find the scene still being played on the large monitor. Pushing open the door to The Room, he looked up to see the disappointing sight of a blank screen showing nothing but the white static of a monitor receiving no signal.

Chapter Fifteen

The week before Christmas was similar to all of the other holiday weeks in a middle school: teachers showing movies and throwing parties, children bringing in candy and getting more and more excitable as the first day of vacation came closer to the present. This had always been James' favorite time of the year. Even though the season brought tremendous levels of stress, he could always look forward to sitting down in the evenings and watching any number of holiday classic movies that had been broadcast around the clock for the past three weeks. With five days until Christmas and only one more day of work before being granted a two week vacation, James decided that tonight he could afford to stay up a little later than usual and indulge in a personal tradition. Each year, normally late at night, one of the cable networks would broadcast the comical 80's revival of Dickens' *A Christmas Carol*. In this remake, the eternal Bill Murray played Scrooge.

James loved over-the-top comedy. Whenever he and Christy took some time to go see a movie at the local cinema, his viewing pleasure would be either anything with explosions or crude humor. Often the couple would go see movies that left them crying from laughing so hard even though the jokes being told were not necessarily of the type that one would sit down and discuss with mom at the dinner table. It was the idea that James and Christy were able to be the perfect man and wife at church on Sunday, raise a great kid and be the perfect parents, and yet have the ability to fit in with society and see hilarity in the crude things of the world that allowed James to enjoy himself so freely. It is the desire of all boys when they are young to lead two lives, one as the perfect all around good guy and the other as an alter ego super hero. James had never really moved beyond this stage in his life. He cared deeply about what others thought about him, although he would never admit it. In the sanctuary of his own house, however, he often did what made him happy. Tonight that meant sitting down in the basement by himself watching *Scrooged*.

It was about midnight when for the twenty-fifth time in his life, James watched the character being portrayed by Bill Murray get visited by The Ghost of Christmas Past. It was this character that usually brought the biggest chuckle to James as he watched a grown man go back and look at events from his past as though he were a third party observer. He smiled broadly as he watched a scene of the young Bill Murray receiving the usual harsh treatment from his dad that led to yet another sarcastic tirade from the modern day man.

James always liked the concept behind the story he was watching. A broken and beaten old man tainted by his past is able to make good on his mistakes by beginning anew and changing his outlook on life. With his feet kicked up and his body reclined on his favorite chair, James once again found himself sitting in the basement with the TV on while his mind wandered to that thing that was beginning to haunt him like his own ghost. He had never realized it until now. The cubby being hidden behind the stairs was serving a purpose similar to the ghosts visiting poor old Ebenezer. Each time he climbed through the door, he was able to witness another scene from his own life as if he were some outside observer. Many times the scenes looked a little bit different than what he remembered, but he was sure that the events were from his own life.

Reaching down and hitting the power button on the remote control, he pulled himself to a standing position and stared at the dark spot under the stairs. Taking two steps closer to the opening, he crouched down and slid into what had become his new private lair.

Entering the room, James was greeted by a new sight. When he looked up at the TV monitor that was placed directly across from him, James expected to see another scene from his childhood. A few months ago that discovery had brought a sense of fear. Today the absence of such a scene left him with a feeling of disappointment. Tonight, instead of broadcasting a scene from his past, the monitor appeared to be broadcasting a live feed. Looking straight ahead, James had a feeling of looking in a mirror. As he took another step closer he saw his image on the screen do the same. Mimicking what every person does when walking through the electronics department at Wal-Mart when they notice they are being taped by a camcorder for sale, James waved his hand as if saying hello to the camera and watched as his image on the screen recreated his movements.

Located on the bottom left corner of the monitor was today's date and time, 12:18 a.m. Dec. 21, along with three initials REC. James assumed this stood for RECORD meaning that this scene too was being recorded only to be shown to him at a later date.

Diverting his glare from the screen, he walked to the stack of DVDs that seemed to be getting larger each day. Over the past two weeks James had spent some time in this room each day. Sometimes he would do nothing more than poke his head through the door to see what part of his past was being broadcast that day. Other times like this one, he would actually spend a great deal more time sifting through the stacks of discs that represented his life, trying to make sense of it all.

Three days ago on Monday he had actually been in there for more than four hours. It wasn't until he heard his wife walking down the stairs to wish him a goodnight and give him a kiss that he even realized where he was. He had gotten himself so engrossed in a scene from a decade earlier that he had completely lost track of the time. Hearing his wife's gentle steps on the stairs above his head had prompted him to come running out of the room and to dive onto his recliner just before she entered. Kissing him on the head, she noticed the small beads of perspiration that were lining his forehead and asked him if everything was all right. He had responded by stating that the stress from working was getting to him and that he just needed the opportunity to take time to himself vegging out in front of the TV forgetting about the day's events. Being the incredible woman that she was, she responded by placing another gentle kiss on his cheek and said, "If sitting in your favorite chair and watching a few sports highlights will help you forget about your day without me so that you can enjoy your night with me, take as much time as you need." And then she walked away.

For the last three nights James had been taking advantage of his wife's generosity by insisting that he was going to take some time to unwind downstairs by watching a movie when in reality he was spending time perusing through The Room's volumes.

Tonight he found himself drawn to the large stack of DVD's just inside The Room's entrance. It was there that he found sleeve upon sleeve of discs with the most recent of dates, including one with yesterday's date and an empty sleeve with today's date. Upon first discovering this room, James had initially been baffled and confused. How anyone could gain access to so many events from his life and capture them all on tape made no sense to him. He had spent many nights lying in bed trying to fall asleep while trying to piece together the nonexistent clues as to who might have been responsible for it all and how they had done it.

Lately, however, he was beginning to experience a new sense of curiosity. It was not that he no longer wondered about the origin of the room. It was just that he no longer dwelled on that aspect. Sure he would love to discover how someone had been able to tap into his memories like they had, but he just didn't obsess with that part of it. Now he found himself almost craving a new adventure each night. He no longer entered The Room with the hope of uncovering some new clue to unravel the mystery. He now entered for the sole purpose of reliving a moment from his past. Since he came to the realization that each scene he was witnessing was indeed a moment of his life caught on camera, he had almost a craving to relive every moment of his life. He did not care what stage of his development he watched just so long as he could watch a stage. He had witnessed events from as early as his first birthday party to events that had taken place at school just a few weeks ago. The thing that intrigued him the most was the fact that the scenes did not seem to be arranged in any kind of chronological order. On the shelves, the movies were always in order and up to the minute, but the images he was able to witness on the screen were always a surprise. He could arrive on one day and watch an event from when he was sixteen. He could close the door and come back five minutes later and then be witness to a brand new scene from ten years later. It was this new mystery that had him coming back for more. It was as if the more his past was broadcast before him, the more he wanted it to be a part of his present.

Flipping through the disks tonight, James let out a sigh as he saw the dates symbolizing last week flip through his fingers. Getting to the bottom of the pile, he was struck by a thought. The absence of a scene on the monitor had left him feeling unfulfilled. He had yet to discover the playback device in The Room so he did not know where the movies were being broadcast from, but he also never really cared. With a desire to watch his past unfold in front of him and no ability to control the monitor now showing only a mirrored reflection of current events, James grabbed three disks at random, shoved them inside the pocket of the ragged robe he had been wearing to keep warm and comfortable while in the basement and walked back out into the open at the bottom of the stairs. Not having a DVD player hooked up to the entertainment system in the Man Room, he ran to the first floor of the house, taking two steps at a time, where he thought he would be able to view images in the family room.

Opening the door at the top of the stairs, James blinked as his eyes were forced to focus in an environment of extreme darkness. Apparently, Christy had turned off all of the lights when she went to bed and the timer that activated the lights on the Christmas tree the family had put up last weekend had not been set properly. Walking to the spot where he believed he would find a switch, James rubbed his hand up and down the wall. Hitting the switch on his third pass he was greeted by the welcome glow of light from a lamp located next to the couch on the other side of the room.

Not wanting to waste any time, he walked over to the entertainment center, sat on one knee, and gently maneuvered through the necessary steps involved with allowing the TV to show a DVD and allowing the DVD player to load the movie. When greeted by the word *Loaded* on the front of the DVD player console, James situated himself on the floor about three feet away from the screen with two remotes in his hands—one that would allow him to adjust the volume settings, and another which would allow him to control the scenes on the disk.

As he wiggled his torso to get into a comfortable position, his right thumb depressed the button that would allow today's, or more appropriately, last week's movie to begin…Then he looked up to see Christy standing at the top of the stairs that led to their bedroom!

With one hand on the guard rail and her body dressed in a set of flannel pajamas James had given her five years ago at Christmas, Christy silently walked to the bottom of the stairs before asking, "What are you doing up here? I thought you were going to watch your movie in the basement so that you wouldn't have to worry about waking Travis when you laughed. You know he's going to wake up if it gets too loud up here."

Without looking down James' right thumb pressed the "stop" button that his mind had memorized the placement of on the remote. He then responded, "I decided to watch a different movie. I don't have a DVD player downstairs so I decided to come up here. I'll be quiet."

Taking a few steps closer, Christy hovered next to her husband and said, "Vacation will be here soon. I guess I can stay up with you. What are we watching?"

Not having thought about this possibility, James paused a moment too long before answering. Before he was able think of the right words to say, Christy had swooped down and stolen the remote controls from his hands and had started pressing the "play" button.

Sitting there for what seemed to be minutes, although in actuality was only about ten seconds, James was terrified. In the short amount of time that he sat there waiting for an image to pop up on the screen literally twenty-five years of his life flashed through his mind. What scene was she going to witness? Sure he had grabbed disks from the pile with lasts week's dates, but he still did not know if that meant these disks would show events from last week or if these disks were simply made and/ or discovered last week. What events from his past had he not yet talked about with her? How would he explain all of this? Maybe, though, he would not have to explain it, because maybe she was behind all of it. It was still a possibility that it was all a part of some big surprise. Although it had not been a part of a birthday surprise, maybe he would be given access to all of the answers to his questions in a couple of days on Christmas… but then again maybe not.

After a silence filled ten seconds Christy stood up. It was then that James realized that there was still no image on the screen. The monitor was full of static.

"Something's not working. Did you push the right buttons to turn on the DVD player?" Christy asked, setting the remote controls down and walking over to the system to try and remedy the problem herself.

Within seconds she did.

"There's no disk in here. You can't watch a DVD without putting one in the DVD player. What were you planning on watching?" she giggled at her husband.

Bewildered, this time James thought quickly. Rubbing his eyes he let out an exaggerated yawn and stated, "I must be tired. I came up here thinking I was going to watch Bill Murray on DVD. I must have fallen asleep while he was on TV downstairs and basically sleepwalked up here. This is kind of embarrassing."

Taking him by his hand, Christy squeezed it lovingly and said, "Let's go to bed. I think you need a good night's sleep and you already have to get up in a couple of hours."

Lying in bed, James was not able to fall asleep. He remained awake throughout the night going over and over that night's events. He knew for a fact that he had grabbed a handful of disks to watch upstairs. He knew he had inserted one into the DVD player. Why had it not shown? Why had Christy not seen the disk in the player? And why had she not seen the stack of DVDs he was sure he had placed on the floor next to him?

Perhaps she had figured out that he found her secret present and wanted to play it off for as long as possible. This was a possibility, but for some reason it just didn't feel very likely.

With vacation less than twenty-four hours away, James once again vowed to figure out the mystery of The Room. This time, though, he gave himself just over a week, as he told himself that by the New Year he had to have all of the answers. Rolling over to look at the clock for the final time before closing his eyes, he did not notice the faint green light beginning to illuminate once again a few inches away, capturing this moment on a tape that would be shelved in the basement along with every other moment of his life.

Chapter Sixteen

The three days that had surrounded Christmas this year were exhausting. Going from one party to the next, shaking hands, and acting interested when discussing work and politics with family members he only saw three times a year, had taken its toll on James. He came home each evening, placed Travis's new presents in his room, got him ready for bed, and soon after crawled under his own king sized comforter. He did not have the time or the energy to do much else. The evening of December twenty-seventh, things finally started to slow down.

With all of the new empty boxes sitting on the curb out front waiting for the trash collectors and all of his new ties hanging in his closet, James was ready to take some time to just sit in his recliner and do nothing. Unfortunately, that is not quite how it worked out.

As he sat in his favorite chair and pressed the power button on the remote control, James looked at the TV screen to see a channel guide that displayed the programs currently being broadcast as well as the date and time.

"The twenty-seventh? Already? I only have six days before I have to go back to work," he muttered to himself while pulling the lever that elevated his legs and feet.

Letting out a deep sigh, he threw a small thin blanket over his torso and shifted his body weight to get into maximum comfort. Before he had even cycled once through all of the available channels afforded to him with his subscription, James was already lost in a deep slumber.

Three hours later James was startled back to consciousness by a tickling sensation on his left cheek. Opening his eyes he saw his wife hovering over him apparently having just placed a gentle kiss on the side of his face. Grinning, he sat up to a more erect posture.

"Hi hon. I just wanted to catch up on a little shuteye. How long have I been out? What time is it?"

Sitting on the arm of the chair, she patted his left leg as she responded, "Well I just put Travis down for the night. I'm not sure when you fell asleep, but you came down here about three hours ago."

"Then I've been asleep for almost three hours. I don't remember anything after turning on the TV. I was in the middle of a weird dream though, so I'm glad you woke me up. Not to mention, if you would have let me sleep much longer I probably wouldn't be able to fall asleep tonight."

Moving her hand to now twirl the long brown hairs by her husbands left ear she continued, "Yeah, well, I debated about what to do. When I started coming down here I could tell you were out because I didn't hear you moving around. When I actually saw you, you looked so peaceful, but then I selfishly thought that if I didn't wake you now, I wouldn't get much sleep tonight either because I would have to put up with your tossing and turning until the wee hours of the morning."

"Well whatever your motivation, I appreciate it. Thanks for

putting the little man down all by yourself too. Did everything go all right?"

Smiling the devilish smile she would display whenever she felt like she was letting someone in on a secret she believed only she knew about she said, "Oh, don't think I wouldn't have been down here a long time ago had he given me any trouble. I know I'm a great wife, but I'm no saint. If he had started crying or getting stubborn with me, I wouldn't have cared how peaceful you looked. I would have been waking you up by placing a fussy little boy in your lap. But, I didn't have too. Instead you can just remember how sweet I am, because of the sweet little kiss I placed on your cheek and my generosity by playing a single parent this evening." Her sarcastic charm had been part of what helped him fall in love with her a decade ago.

Grinning back, James grabbed his wife's hand that was back resting on his leg and said, "All of my memories of you are great. It doesn't matter what really happens, all I can ever remember is the good stuff you do for me. I try my best to blot out any bad stuff from my past. Isn't that what marriage is all about? I'm sure you do the same thing. But then again I have never really screwed up. I really am always good. It must be a lot easier for you to filter your memories." He knew that she always got a kick out of it when he attempted sarcastic humor back at her.

"Is that what I am supposed to do? I wish someone would have told me that five years ago. I have been holding a grudge against you for years for that time you put the toilet paper back on the roll with the paper coming from over the top." She giggled before continuing. "I'm just kidding. You are pretty good. I'm a lucky lady. I truly do believe you married down when you chose me, but I am grateful."

"You know life is all about sacrifice," James said laughing through each word.

"Well I am going to head off to bed now. Will you wait and come up when you are fairly confident that you will actually be able to fall asleep?" Christy asked as she bent down to place another kiss on her husband, this time on his forehead.

"Sure. I'm not sure how long I'll be, but I'll be up eventually," he said while squeezing her hand just a little bit tighter before releasing it completely so that she could head up the stairs.

As soon as he heard his wife close the door at the top of the stairs, he was up and walking towards The Room. He hadn't forgotten that he made a vow to himself to solve the mysteries surrounding everything under the stairs by the end of the year, but lately he hadn't had the time to do much more than think about what he had seen over the past couple of months. His thoughts had not availed much.

Tonight, for example, as he slept in his comfy brown chair his mind played a scene that was not quite a moment from his past, but a dream that was more like realistic fiction. He experienced the time when he and his wife first met each other and the events that led up to their becoming a couple, including their first time spending a holiday together. In reality, the two of them had met up in college and had spent a full year as a couple before ever venturing to take the major step of introducing the other person to each one's extended family.

James was the first guinea pig. Christy had convinced him to come visit her at the cabin her parents owned on a lake in the northern part of the state over the Fourth of July weekend. James normally stayed on the college campus during the summer working and taking classes, but this year she begged him to make a statement of his commitment to her by coming to see her.

The weekend had actually been pretty relaxing. Along with her parents and sister, James was given the opportunity to meet two of her aunts, two uncles, and the six nieces and nephews that belonged to the couples. Amazingly while there he never once experienced a moment of awkward silence and genuinely liked the people. It was that weekend that had confirmed for him that Christy would be the woman he would marry.

The dream he had tonight showed the scene differently. The holiday was not the Fourth, but Christmas Day. The people present were not members of Christy's family, but a conglomerate of friends the two had shared in college. Most shocking of all, the woman he was visiting was not Christy, but one of her roommates—a girl named Anne.

He was already having a difficult time remembering all of the details of the dream, but he knew that he had experienced an extremely awkward feeling when being awakened by his wife. When greeted by the soft kiss of the woman he had been married to for approximately a decade, he actually thought the kiss was coming from Anne. Seeing his wife sitting next to him and sharing a tender moment of laughter with her had made him feel very uncomfortable. Throughout the entire conversation he had just had, he was unable to fully concentrate on the words the couple was exchanging. Instead, he felt more like Eddie Haskell from *Leave it to Beaver*. He was overplaying his insecurity. Not wanting Christy to ask what he was dreaming about, or even worse to be able to tell what he was thinking about simply by looking at him like she was sometimes inclined to do, he tried to sell the idea of him being the world's best husband, her being the best wife, and together they were in turn the perfect couple.

Now that his wife was gone, he decided it was time to once again return to the room that housed so much of his life. He did not expect to see the scene that he had just dreamed about, but the thoughts of his past had once again raised up in him a desire to explore.

The scene he was being shown tonight was difficult to focus on at first. Instead of being derived from a stationary camera located in some obscure location in the room he was in, the camera that had produced these images was moving and bouncing around tremendously. A few years ago, he and Christy had rented a horror movie supposedly filmed by amateur filmmakers out in the woods as they were chased and murdered in the middle of the night. This tape reminded him of that. He could not easily make out the characters in the movie or even easily hear the conversation that was being broadcast through the monitor's speakers.

It was about three minutes into the video that James came to the realization that the camera that had been used had apparently been placed into someone's bag or purse. The swaying motion and the straps that could sometimes be seen in the upper corners of the screen gave him that opinion. It was about a minute later that he realized exactly what he was witnessing. It was the Fourth of July, but it was not the weekend in which he had ultimately realized his love for his future wife. This was the year after. The year that he realized that he was a despicable man. This particular weekend was the weekend in which an event had taken place that he had never discussed with Christy.

Christy had once again gone to her parents' cabin. This time she went for the sole purpose of showing off the new two-carat diamond she had on the fourth finger of her left hand. James had proposed to her the week before and she intended to brag about him to everybody. Unfortunately James was not able to make the trip. He had plans to graduate at the end of the summer term and in order for that to become a reality, he would have to stay on campus and study for his upcoming exams.

On the night of the Fourth, James received a phone call from Christy who called to check up on him. The video had begun with a scene about a half an hour later.

James had been in his apartment typing up some of his notes for his biology class when he heard a knock at the door. Standing in the hall when he opened the door were two of Christy's roommates—Anne and Nicole. Both were dressed in short skirts and spaghetti strapped tops. Anne carried a small purse. The girls had come over, as they explained, because Christy had just called them and asked them to stop by and invite him out so that he could relax just a little bit and enjoy the holiday. He explained to the girls that he couldn't leave, but they were welcome to come in. Nicole explained that she was expected to meet her boyfriend at a party so she could not stay, but Anne took him up on the offer.

She and James then spent the next two hours sitting on the couch talking. The conversation was not deep or profound, but he had been focused on every detail.

As the conversation continued, James noticed from the video the body language of the two of them grew more and more relaxed. When Anne first came in, James had offered her a bottle of whatever cheap beer he had in his refrigerator. Now there were a total of six empty bottles littering the table around where both of them had reclined their feet.

It was at this point that Anne decided that it was time for her to get going. She explained that Nicole would be extremely worried if she did not show up soon. James sprung to his feet and reached out his arms to help Anne rise out of the soft sofa sleeper the two had been virtually stuck in for one hundred twenty minutes. Grabbing her hands and pulling her towards him, James watched as his former self then leaned in and kissed Anne with an open mouth.

It was a brief kiss, but a monumental kiss. Escorting her to the door, James lowered his head and made a sincere apology. With a sweet smile Anne shook her head causing her blonde hair to bounce slightly and explained that it was okay. She had wanted him to kiss her and could have pulled away. The two agreed that it would be their own little secret and she hustled away into the hallway. Seconds later, the screen went to static.

Because the video had been shown in real time, James had truly been in The Room for more than two hours. Tuning out the static from the screen, James instinctively looked around him. If Christy ever got her hands on this video, she would be furious. Realizing that she was not there with him, he began to understand that there was no way Christy had been responsible for obtaining all of the footage he had watched down there. There was no way she would have been able to see what he had just seen and not responded to it.

Now he focused on a new question. *Should I tell my wife not only about The Room, but about the scenes being broadcast therein?*

Chapter Seventeen

It was tradition at Divine Hope Church to host a New Year's Eve service every December 31st. As James and Christy dropped Travis off in the nursery, the couple discussed how strange it would be for the two of them to sit in on a service together. Because it was a special service, there was no need for an ushering staff so James would be able to sit next to his wife and listen to an entire sermon.

As the choir wrapped up its final song and the members of the congregation returned to their seats, James was brought back into reality as Christy grabbed his hand and pulled him down next to her. While the church had been engaged in singing a few songs that James would never again be able to identify, he was deep in thought trying desperately to piece together the answers to the questions he now had less than an hour to solve. A few days ago, he made a commitment to himself that if he had not stumbled upon a solution to The Room he would share all of it, including what was in each video, with his wife.

Although he had not been in for a full service since this time last year, James always appreciated his pastor's speaking ability. He remembered how last year at this service, Pastor John had delivered a message about the importance of goal setting and the relevance of setting New Year's resolutions. He spoke about reading the Bible every day, and spending quiet time in prayer each morning. James had left that service inspired and motivated. He, along with 150 others, had even signed a contract with the church to do just those things for the entire year that followed. James breached the contract by the middle of February and as his discussions with others had proven, most of the others had too.

Tonight Pastor John was just getting started, but was already being greeted by the welcome cry of "Amen" and "That's right" by some of the church's elders and leaders.

Five minutes into the message, James heard a statement that again made him aware of his surroundings. "The greatest present you can give your loved ones during this holiday season is to forget your past. That is the title of tonight's message, *The present is not your past.*"

James had heard about people who claimed that they had heard messages from God—people who claimed that God had given them visions and prophesies. James had even been one of those people who believed in such tales for the first few years of his life as a member of Divine Hope. When he and his wife had to spend five years trying to get pregnant, however, he had given up on the idea of God communicating with, or even being concerned about, the day-to-day happenings of people on earth. He believed in God and the powers usually associated with him, but with the exception of the six weeks at the beginning of last year, James just did not believe it mattered to God what he did on a daily basis, as long as he was generally a good person.

As Pastor John continued through his talk, he made statements that really hit James hard. "Many people will tell you that it is important to study history. Without learning from our past, we will be condemned to repeat our mistakes." James had made the same statement to classes of kids back when he was in the classroom on a daily basis. "This is not a Biblical principal," Pastor John continued. "Jesus taught to turn the other cheek. In other words forget about the pain the person just caused you and allow it to happen again. He did not tell us to learn to duck and weave. He taught us to forget about it and move on. We read in Second Peter, chapter one, verse nine, that we have been cleansed from our past. We do not need to dwell on it.

"Many times during this time of year, we are hit by the nostalgia bug. We look back at our lives. We celebrate accomplishments and we think of all of the things we still want to do while here on this earth. Last year at this service, I encouraged everyone to look at the future and do exactly what I just condemned. I wanted you to think about where you have fallen short in the past and come up with a plan to correct it. I apologize for that. What I directed you to do was not in line with the will of God. In order for me to direct you in the will of God, I sometimes need to make statements that are not popular and go against popular tradition.

"Tonight I do not want you to make resolutions. I do not want you to think about your failures. I want you to focus on where you are right now. Right now you have the ability to enjoy a relationship with your Father. He does not care what you have done or what you will do. He cares for you right now."

As Pastor John continued on, James found his head swirling. Twenty minutes ago, he could not focus on the choir singing fifteen feet in front of him because he was too busy recalling events from fifteen years ago. Now he was being told that his past did not matter. Perhaps Pastor John was right. Perhaps the past was just a distraction. After all, it had forced him to tune out the beautiful service going on around him. It had caused him to become distant from his wife and now he was even struggling with being honest with her. How, though, was he supposed to just forget about what happened to him? How was he supposed to avoid the temptation of visiting The Room and witnessing his life all over again?

Glancing to his left to where his wife was seated next to him, James noticed that Christy had her head bowed and her eyes closed. Closing his own eyes in quick response, James again listened to the voice emanating from behind the pulpit.

"Before we pray I want you to remember this one thought. Those of you who have a personal relationship with Jesus always have Him with you. He has been with you since the moment you asked Him into your life. He has witnessed your good times and your bad times. He has stood beside you through moments where you felt like you were drowning in the sea of life. He has access to your most intimate thoughts. He taught us that He and His father would forgive us of all of our actions. This is the creator of the world we are talking about. He was with you in your past and He has chosen not to hold it against you. Why do you?

"Tonight I want you to say a personal prayer to God. Ask Him to forgive you for your past and then ask Him to help you turn from it. Ask that He allow you to focus on the present and not dwell on the past. If this is something you are willing to do, I will give you the next minute or two to talk to God. Tell Him what's on your mind and then we will all move forward and count down the New Year together."

Five minutes later, after both having said the prayer prompted by Pastor John, James and Christy found themselves alone in the back of the sanctuary. The rest of the crowd had gathered towards the front near the pastor and his wife to retrieve noisemakers and party hats that were being passed out. James had mentioned to his wife that he wanted to talk to her and had requested that the two of them hang back for a minute so he could share something with her.

After completing his prayer, James determined that the only way for him to finally move beyond his past was to explain all that he had witnessed in his basement. With only five minutes until the crystal ball dropped on Time's Square in New York City there was no way he would come up with a suitable explanation before his self imposed deadline.

He began, "Christy, Pastor John's message really got to me tonight. You know you and I have gone through a lot, but there are some things I haven't told you about."

"James Daniel Carlise. I am ashamed of you. You just said that Pastor's message really got to you and then you want to start reliving things from your past. Didn't you hear a word he said?"

"Yeah, of course I did, but listen. There's something you should know."

Smiling her devilish smile again she questioned, "Does it concern how much you love me or how great you think I am? If not I am not interested. I really appreciated what I heard tonight and I want to live in my present."

"Okay. I'll respect that. If you won't let me talk to you now, will you make me a promise? Tonight when we get home, not tomorrow morning, tonight, will you come into the basement with me so I can show you something?"

"I'll promise you that if you promise me that what you want to show me concerns the present, because that is all I care about tonight."

Winking at her and grabbing her right hand as the crowd in front of them began the chant of *ten...nine...eight*, he said, "I promise you it is something here and now."

Chapter Eighteen

With Travis sound asleep in his crib, James guided his wife down the stairs that led to the basement. On their way down he explained, "What I'm going to show you is something that has been puzzling me for months. I have been debating whether or not to share this with you, but now I know that you are the only one who can help shed some light on everything. I'll point you in the right direction and then let you stumble into it like I did so I can see your initial reaction. It's going to be a shock. I'm warning you.

"I first noticed this months ago when you asked me to bring Travis's stuff down here to store."

Letting go of his hand she asked, "What am I looking for?"

Bending down into a squatted position, he pointed under the stairs, "Back there against that wall. See what you can find."

Obeying her husband's request and fulfilling her promise to look into whatever was causing him so much worry, she climbed into the cubby and disappeared into the darkness with the exception of her feet which were still sticking out from the spot in which she had just entered. Ten seconds later, she was back standing next to her husband. "What was that?"

Nodding his head he replied, "I don't know. That is why

I brought you down here. I was hoping you could offer an explanation."

"Well my opinion is that it is a spider's nest. I know you hate spiders, so I'll take care of it. You know if you first noticed it months ago, you should have told me about it then."

"Yeah, that's real manly—me screaming for you to run downstairs to kill some spiders because I'm too scared."

"I know you're macho and don't want to admit you're scared, but who knows how many spiders have been born in there. But I do not want to dwell on the past. First thing tomorrow I'll come down with the vacuum and suck that thing up," she said.

Perplexed James asked, "What are you talking about? Didn't you see that door? It sticks a little, but if you push hard you can get it open. It's all the way in the back."

"James honey it'll be okay. I know you're scared and embarrassed. There's no door back there and I know that you would have never crawled back far enough to discover if there was a door with that big of a nest hanging in there. I'm going to bed now. Travis will be up at his regular time and one of us needs to be coherent."

This time James did not wait for Christy to disappear up the stairs before diving under them to get to the door of The Room. Halfway there, he looked directly in front of him to where the door should have been but it wasn't. The only thing there, just as Christy had described it, was an enormous nest. Back pedaling on his knees James retreated to a spot next to his recliner.

"What in the world?" he mumbled. "What happened to The Room? What happened to my past? It couldn't have just been sealed up while we were at church tonight. There's no way a spider could have just built that nest today. Christy is going to think I'm crazy if I tell her about this now."

Sitting down in his chair and elevating his feet into his normal position, he tried to make sense of what was going on. Reclining there, thinking about all he had witnessed over the past eight months from the little green lights turning up everywhere he went, to the videos of his childhood, college years, and his days at the office, to the mysterious disappearing of it all, he was baffled trying to come up with a logical explanation.

Being startled awake by the sound of the vacuum, James opened his eyes and noticed light creeping into the glass block windows located above his TV and realized he was still in the basement sitting in his chair. Pressing the switch to turn off the vacuum, Christy walked over to her husband, rubbed her fingers through his hair and said, "There you go honey. Everything you have been worried about for the past few months is now gone. Now you can hang out down here and not have to worry about being confronted with your biggest fear. Its all in the past now. Happy New Year."

Afterword

James Carlise is a fictional character. Although designed and created from my own imagination, he is meant to represent more that just a man. He is meant to represent EVERY man.

Personally I am in many ways similar to James. At the time of writing this, I too am an educator in a large public school. I am an usher at my local church. I have a beautiful wife and a wonderful fourteen-month old son. However, James was not created to simply play my persona in a story.

To be honest, it has been my desire for years to write a book, but never a novel. I have begun multiple books in the past all dealing with various aspects of wisdom or self-improvement. Unfortunately soon after starting each, I found myself at a loss. No book could move beyond the first few pages, maybe because I am still lacking in wisdom or knowledge. Finally early last year, I decided to put the idea of writing on hold for a while. It was at that point that the storyline for this book came to me.

I had no idea how to write a fictional story, but for some reason creating the plot for this book came relatively easy. There were a few times where I found myself stuck and I would respond the same way I always did, by simply putting the writing process on hold. With this book, however, something unusual always happened. Each time I would decide to stop writing, within a few days I would wake up in the morning with the next few chapters outlined in my head.

A few weeks ago I came to the point where I thought this book was all done. I printed off the "completed" manuscript and sent it off to a few publishers with hopes of getting a deal. In no time at all, I received phone calls and e-mails telling me that publishing companies actually liked it and would love to reproduce the story.

Last night, however, while contemplating a few of the offers before me, I once again came to the realization that this book was not done. There is more to write. That is what I have here. Although the elements to the story that you just read were designed to entertain and engage your thinking by showing you a glimpse of a fictional character, I now believe it is important to explain why I believe this story came so naturally and easily.

As I stated earlier, James represents EVERY man, not just me, not just you. Every man knows what it is like to face temptations on a wide variety of levels. Every man knows the pressures associated with trying to maintain a good reputation, a quality family, and individual success. James is a man who spent much of his early adult life just trying to make it through each day while balancing all aspects of his life and trying to keep his priorities in order. One thing, however, was keeping him from his full potential to be the man he was created to be: his own selfish pride. It was his pride that kept him from asking his wife for help in solving the mystery surrounding him. It was pride that drove him to sit around for hours on end exploring the mistakes of his past. It was pride that drove him to think he could handle everything on his own. It was pride that brought him so much concern about someone watching him and actually being able to view his thoughts and motivations.

This is the way it is for most men. It is my belief that the only thing that keeps any of us from being perfect is pride. If it were not for our own pride we would never think that we could get away with doing anything contrary to what God has instructed us to do. It is our pride that often tempts us to think that we can fix everything on our own. Our own arrogance has become the thing that separates us from God.

I am always hesitant to try and convince people about the realities of God by referencing the Bible, as many who deny His existence do so because they do not believe that the Bible is truth to begin with; but whether you see the Bible as no more than a book of stories designed to teach moral awareness or as the Word of God, we can see multiple examples of this being proven true and the story of James Carlise being explained.

Satan (the devil) for example was created to be one of God's angels. He, however, began to think that he could do things on his own. He did not think he needed God's approval or blessing, so he began to swell with pride. His pride eventually got him kicked out of Heaven and sent to earth.

King David began his assent to the throne by being the young boy who had the courage to kill the mighty giant Goliath, with nothing more than a sling shot. Once he became king, however, his pride and arrogance led him to commit adultery and murder.

Most of us have not gotten to the point of committing sins so grievous, but I believe it is safe to say we all have moments in our lives that, if we were given the opportunity to do so, we would like to go back and fix. We all have tainted pasts.

Some people have the belief that if they are not perfect, there is no hope for them. Other people take the other extreme and argue that you can behave however you want and still get to Heaven as long as you say a simple prayer and take a mysterious walk down the aisle of a church and cry a little. Both of these positions are what I believe have given Christians around the world such a bad reputation. We are seen as either hypocrites or radicals. Most are not seen as examples or people to be followed. I would argue that anyone who believes that either of the above positions are correct face just as much turmoil as someone who lives in the remote jungles of Africa and has never even heard the name Jesus.

In James's situation, he was haunted by his past. He did not commit any crime that would get him thrown into prison. He did not abandon his wife or child. For some reason, however, he was still plagued by his past failures. This is how it is for a lot of us. When he finally came to the point in his life however, when he realized he needed help to sift through his past, it was gone. He no longer had access to his memories. He came to the point where he asked God to help him move beyond his past, and it was done. He could no longer view his mistakes. His wife could not get access to events that may have caused her emotional harm. It was all gone. I believe that this was his saving moment.

I do not believe salvation is something that is given to anyone who simply believes that Jesus existed. If that were true, satan would be in Heaven. He and all of his demons believe in Jesus. Satan has even had conversations with Him (Luke chapter 4). Satan however is bound for hell, not Heaven.

Likewise, simply living a good life will not get you into

Heaven. As I ask my students in my classroom when they have been caught doing something wrong, "What is worse: driving five miles per hour over the speed limit or ten miles per hour?"

They, of course, always answer, "Ten miles per hour."

I then ask, "Which person did something illegal?"

The answer once again is always unanimous "They both did."

It is the same thing with us. We try to justify ourselves by comparing the wrong we have done to the wrongs others have done, but the bottom line is we have all done wrong. If Heaven is a place that is perfect, with no sickness, disease, despair, or death; then NO sin can enter. Sin is sin. Wrong is wrong. God does not act like the ancient Egyptian sun god and place our hearts on a scale and measure it against a feather to determine if out hearts are too heavy to be in Heaven.

I do not profess to have all of the answers. As a matter of fact, the next book I am planning to write is going to be simply a list of questions I still have for God. But I do know this, God has made a plan for us to get into Heaven even though we are not perfect. It is this: believe in His Son, Jesus Christ. This does not mean believe He existed, but believe He is who He said He is and that He can do what He said He can do.

I have two examples to demonstrate this point. The first deals with multiple stories in the first four books of the New Testament (The Gospels). Multiple times in these books, Jesus explains to people who He is talking to that the path to Heaven is a difficult one. There was one specific man who approached Him and asked what he had to do to become one of His disciples. Jesus responded by telling the man, who was very wealthy, to get rid of all of his possessions immediately and follow Him. As a matter of fact, that is what He told all of his disciples. Some He even instructed not go say goodbye to their families. In order to be with Him, Jesus instructed these men to remove any semblance of their past. Simply acknowledging Jesus as the Son of God was not enough. He wanted men who were willing to act like they believed He was the Son of God, men who would make Him their priority.

The second example is one a little easier for me to relate to. I have a son. I know I have a son because I can see him and interact with him. I believe he exists. However when he grows up and begins to try new things, simply believing he exists will not be enough support to nurture him. He needs to know that I believe IN him. He needs to know that I believe he is capable of anything. That if he said he can do something, I believe he will succeed at it.

This is what I think is meant in the New Testament when it is written that if you believe in the Lord Jesus you will be saved (Acts 16:31). If my son decides to play basketball and my idea of supporting him involves me telling him one time, "I believe you are on the team," then I have offered him no assurance of my value in him. If, however, I go to his games, cheer him on, practice with him, build him up, and tell him often how impressed I am, then perhaps he will know I believe in him.

Simply saying "I believe in Jesus" does not make a person a Christian. A Christian is a person, according to the actual meaning of the word, who emulates Christ. If you want to be a person who is blessed with the opportunity to live with God and His Son, you must first acknowledge that you believe in Them and then attempt to live like you believe that They are the all knowing-all seeing God. God knows what you are up to at all times. He knows when you mess up. He is your "little green light" watching you at all times. He, however, is also capable of deleting His memory of our mistakes if only we ask Him to.

Do not become a man like James Carlise and try to cover up your past or get worked up by the idea of being watched at all times. God knows that at times we will mess up. When it happens, suppress your pride and ask God to forgive you. Ask Him to help you work on your present and you will be surprised how distant the past appears to you.

About the Author

Dave Schmittou is a teacher in a large suburban school district outside of Detroit, Michigan. Along with his wife, Rachel, he spends the majority of his free time playing with and raising his son, Cameron. *Omniscient* is the first novel Dave has written, but not necessarily the first book concept he has had. At the publication of this book, he is hard at work on a couple of non-fiction titles that he hopes will challenge his readers and bring them to a closer relationship with their Father in the future.

As is mentioned in the afterword of this book, the main character, James Carlise, although not an autobiographical character, was inspired by Dave's own life. He too was raised in a military household. He believes integrity should be the focal point of every man's life and he tries to lead a life as to set an example to all that see him...even to those he is not aware are watching him. It is his goal to lead a life worthy of imitation.

To be Christian means to be Christ-like. He believes that if he lives a life of a true Christian and others then imitate his character, he has indirectly led people to a life closer to the Lord. It is this desire that has allowed him to freely share his faith with his spoken words, and now, on the written page.

Questions and comments are always welcome as Dave enjoys teaching others and sharing his ideas with young and old alike.

To order additional copies of *Omniscient*, or to find out about other books by David Schmittou or Zoë Life Publishing, please visit our website www.zoelifepub.com.

A bulk discount is available when 12 or more books are purchased at one time.

Contact Outreach at Zoë Life Publishing:

Zoë Life Publishing
P.O. Box 871066
Canton, MI 48187
(877) 841-3400
outreach@zoelifepub.com

ZOË LIFE
PUBLISHING
WORDS TO LIVE BY